# Paddington On Stage

*Paddington On Stage* is based on the play *The Adventures Of Paddington Bear* which is in turn based on the original stories by Michael Bond. The full Acting Edition of this play is published by Samuel French Ltd.

*Also by Michael Bond*

A Bear Called Paddington
More About Paddington
Paddington Abroad
Paddington at Large
Paddington at Work
Paddington Goes to Town
Paddington Helps Out
Paddington Marches On
Paddington Takes the Air
Paddington Takes to TV
Paddington on Top

# Paddington On Stage

ADAPTED BY ALFRED BRADLEY
AND MICHAEL BOND

*With drawings by Peggy Fortnum*

HOUGHTON MIFFLIN COMPANY BOSTON 1977

*Paddington on Stage* is based on the play *The Adventures of Paddington Bear*, which is published in a full Acting Edition by Samuel French Ltd.

**Library of Congress Cataloging in Publication Data**

Bradley, Alfred, playwright.
  Paddington on stage.

  A collection of seven short plays based on
M. Bond's play The adventures of Paddington.
  SUMMARY: Plays featuring the Peruvian bear
and his antics in England with the Brown family.
Includes hints for props, sets, and costumes.
    1. Children's plays. |1. Bears—Drama.
  2. Plays| I. Bond, Michael, joint author.
  II. Fortnum, Peggy. III. Bond, Michael. The
adventures of Paddington. IV. Title.
PN6120.A4B67   1977        822'.9'14        76-62497
ISBN 0-395-25155-9

# Contents

*Introduction*                                        7

*Costume Notes*                                       9

1. The Arrival of Paddington                         13

2. Paddington Paints a Picture                       31

3. Paddington Has a Birthday                         45

4. Paddington Visits the Dentist                     57

5. Paddington Goes to the Launderette                67

6. Paddington Goes to the Hospital                   77

7. Paddington Turns Detective                        93

*Songs*                                             109

Over the years lots of children have written in asking "Why isn't there a Paddington play?", and as many again have told of their efforts in schools, or at home in the spare room, the garage, or outside in the garden, to put on a play of their own.

Towards the end of 1973 the first group were catered for when *The Adventures of a Bear Called Paddington* opened at the Nottingham Playhouse.

*Paddington On Stage* is meant for those who like to "do-it-themselves". It's really a selection of playlets from the professional version with all the complicated trimmings – the sets, the props, and some of the more difficult dialogue taken out. You can add to it, take away from it, even make up your own words as you go along; no-one, least of all Paddington, will mind in the slightest.

In short, it's for all children who like to dress-up, play make-believe, or simply have fun – with or without an audience, and to whom a board with two words painted on it turns a room into Paddington Station, and someone wearing an old hat and some wellington boots (plus maybe a duffle-coat if there's one around) becomes Paddington himself.

*Michael Bond.*

# Costume Notes

If you already know the Paddington books, or have read these plays, then you will probably have a picture in your mind's eye of what the main characters look like and how to act them.

It's really very simple: MR and MRS BROWN are the kind of people who *would* take a bear home to live with them. That is to say, they are warm-hearted and rather vague.

MR BROWN is a little less happy about the whole thing than his wife, but only because he feels there may be a law against it. He works in a city office, and this can be suggested by having him carry a rolled umbrella and a folded newspaper when he leaves home; also a briefcase if one is available. He would also wear a hat – a bowler is ideal – but a dark trilby is almost as good. He can have a moustache and glasses – lots of toy or joke shops stock this kind of thing, but a pair of old, unwanted sunglasses with the plastic lenses taken out would be fine. His chin can be darkened slightly with the aid of burnt cork, and age can be suggested by drawing in the "crow's feet" around the eyes with an eyebrow pencil or a black felt pen. The easiest way to find these lines is to stand in front of a mirror, screw up your eyes, then relax them again. But always remember it is better to have too little make-up than too much.

MRS BROWN is well-dressed without being too smart. If you are able to borrow a wig or hair-piece it will help, but even combing your own hair a different way can make a lot of difference to your appearance. She should wear a little make-up, some lipstick and rouge, but again not too much.

The Browns have two children, JONATHAN and JUDY. They are both at school, and secretly rather proud of having a bear about the house. They are also slightly envious of Paddington's ability to get into a mess and still come out on top. As a contrast to the other characters they can wear school clothes.

MRS BIRD, the housekeeper, is older than the Browns and on the surface much more stern. But deep down she is just as soft-hearted and would protect Paddington through thick and thin. She would normally wear her hair in a bun, and it can be made grey, or even white, by combing in some talcum powder. Very pale make-up on the lips is another way of suggesting age. An effective white wig can be made by gluing cotton wool to an old shower cap. She would wear a fairly long skirt, and perhaps a shawl.

Paddington's friend, MR GRUBER, who keeps an antique shop in the Portobello Road, is himself an immigrant from Central Europe, so he has a special relationship with Paddington and understands how it feels to live in a country which isn't really your own. They have a great respect for each other and always use their surnames. He also wears glasses, but steel-rimmed if possible, perched on the end of his nose so that he can look over the top. He walks with a slight stoop and speaks with a hint of a foreign accent. His clothes can be well-worn, comfortable without being down-at-heel.

Last, but not least, is MR CURRY, the Browns' neighbour. He has a reputation for being bad-tempered, with a way of barking out commands rather than holding a conversation. He doesn't approve of Paddington's "goings-on" and never loses an opportunity of telling him so. He should be played "tight-lipped", and with a habit of drawing in his breath as if he is about to explode at any moment.

As suggested in the foreword, PADDINGTON himself can be played by someone dressed in a duffle-coat, wellington boots, and a battered old 1920's style hat. If you have a willing parent, who is also handy with a needle and thread, it might even be possible to make a costume out of some suitable material, but as Paddington is the sort of bear who happily wears his duffle-coat at all times, this is not as important as it might be. (He doesn't actually have it when he is found on Paddington Station, but for the plays this point could be overlooked – it's what is known as "dramatic licence!") He has a strong sense of right and wrong, and a "hard stare" which he often uses when he is upset by something. This could be "pointed" by someone behind the scenes "pinging" a ruler on the edge of a desk. His voice is best played as you hear it in your own head; perhaps a rather high-pitched but gruff voice, if such a thing exists!

There is no need to have a stage as such, or even curtains – lots of theatres nowadays have gone back to the open stage, but if the acting area can have more light than the part where the audience are sitting, then so much the better. At the back of the book you will find the words of two songs from the original stage production. The first *I Try So Hard* can be sung by Paddington himself as an alternative ending for any of the plays other than the first one where it's best if he simply falls asleep. The second song *Paddington Bear* can be used to round off the final play instead of *For He's a Jolly Good Bear Cub*. It will also add a professional touch to have some suitable music on a record player at the beginning and end, and during scene changes or intervals. If the scene changes are done in front of the audience, then fun can be had by doing it in time to the music and turning it into a part of the production. The actors themselves can help out, and if it's well done you may even get a round of applause for that too!

# The Arrival of Paddington

# CAST OF CHARACTERS

MR BROWN
MRS BROWN
PADDINGTON BEAR
REFRESHMENT MAN
JUDY BROWN
MRS BIRD
JONATHAN BROWN

## PROPS

*At Paddington Station:*
Cardboard boxes
Sign saying "Paddington Station"
Suitcase
Jar of marmalade – almost empty
Tea trolley or tray
*Cakes on paper plates
Plastic or paper cups
Drinking straw
*Cake wrapper

*At Number thirty-two, Windsor Gardens:*
Table and chairs
Tray with teapot and cups
Towel
Possibly some cushions and anything
else that helps make the set look like
the Browns' living room.

The play starts on Paddington Station. All that we need is a heap of parcels to hide PADDINGTON, (cardboard boxes will do) and a sign saying "Paddington Station". PADDINGTON wears a floppy bush hat, wellington boots and has a label tied round his neck which says "Please look after this bear. Thank you." In his suitcase, which he takes with him wherever he goes, is a jar of marmalade. When the refreshment man arrives he should have a tea trolley or a tray with several plastic or paper cups and some sticky cakes. *(As real cakes may be messy, it is probably best to make your own using Krazy Foam or shaving cream which will wash off easily.) *The sticky cake wrapper can be made out of an ordinary cake wrapper, covered on both sides with double-sided, transparent sticky tape.

When we get to Number thirty-two, Windsor Gardens we will need a table, and some chairs. You can make the splashing and banging for Paddington's shower by hammering on something noisy (an old biscuit tin would do) and by splashing water in a bucket.

# Scene One

When the play begins PADDINGTON is concealed behind
an assorted pile of parcels and luggage. HENRY BROWN
comes on to the platform, closely followed by his wife.

MR BROWN     Well, Mary, after all that rushing about,
we're here early.

MRS BROWN     What's the time now?

MR BROWN     It's just a quarter past four and Judy's train
doesn't arrive until half past.

MRS BROWN     Are you sure?

MR BROWN     She told me in her letter and she doesn't
usually make mistakes.

MRS BROWN     I'll just go and check which platform . . .
[goes off]

[Left to himself MR BROWN strolls around the platform.
PADDINGTON, hidden behind the parcels, pops up like a
jack-in-the-box and quickly down again. MR BROWN is
looking surprised; MRS BROWN returns]

MRS BROWN     It's platform five. And you're quite right,
the train doesn't arrive until half past four.

MR BROWN     Mary, you won't believe this, but I've just
seen a bear.

MRS BROWN     A what?

MR BROWN     A bear.

MRS BROWN     A bear? On Paddington Station. Don't be
silly, Henry. There can't be.

MR BROWN     But there is. I distinctly saw it. Over there.
Behind those parcels. It was wearing a funny
kind of hat. Come and see for yourself.

MRS BROWN      [*humouring him*] Very well. [*She peers behind the parcels*] Why Henry, I believe you were right after all. It is a bear!

[PADDINGTON *stands up suddenly. He is wearing a bush hat with a wide brim and has a large luggage label round his neck*]

PADDINGTON      Good afternoon. [*He raises his hat*]

MR BROWN      Er . . . good afternoon.

PADDINGTON      Can I help you?

MR BROWN      Well . . . no. Er, not really. As a matter of fact, we were wondering if we could help you.

MRS BROWN      [*taking a closer look*] You're a very unusual bear.

PADDINGTON      I'm a very rare sort of bear. There aren't many of us left where I come from.

MR BROWN      And where is that?

PADDINGTON      Darkest Peru. I'm not really supposed to be here at all. I'm a stowaway.

MRS BROWN      A stowaway?

PADDINGTON      Yes. I emigrated you know. I used to live with my Aunt Lucy in Peru, but she had to go into a Home for Retired Bears.

MRS BROWN      You don't mean to say you've come all the way from South America by yourself?

PADDINGTON      Yes. Aunt Lucy always said she wanted me to emigrate when I was old enough. That's why she taught me to speak English.

MR BROWN      But whatever did you do for food? You must be starving.

PADDINGTON [*opening his suitcase and taking out an almost empty jar*] I ate marmalade. Bears like marmalade. And I hid in a lifeboat.

MR BROWN But what are you going to do now? You can't just sit on Paddington Station waiting for something to happen.

PADDINGTON Oh, I shall be all right . . . I expect.

MRS BROWN What does it say on your label?

MR BROWN [*reading it*] "Please look after this bear. Thank you."

MRS BROWN That must be from his Aunt Lucy. Oh, Henry, what shall we do? We can't just leave him here. There's no knowing what might happen to him. Can't he come and stay with us for a few days?

MR BROWN But Mary, dear, we can't take him . . . not just like that. After all . . .

MRS BROWN After all, what? He'd be good company for Jonathan and Judy. Even if it's only for a little while. They'd never forgive us if they knew you'd left him here.

MR BROWN It all seems highly irregular. I'm sure there's a law against it. [*Turning to* PADDINGTON] Would you like to come and stay with us? That is, if you've nothing else planned.

PADDINGTON [*overjoyed*] Oooh, yes, please. I should like that very much. I've nowhere to go and everyone seems in such a hurry.

MRS BROWN Well, that's settled then. And you can have marmalade for breakfast every morning . . .

PADDINGTON   Every morning? I only had it on special occasions at home. Marmalade's very expensive in Darkest Peru.

MRS BROWN   Then you shall have it every morning starting tomorrow.

PADDINGTON   [*worried*] Will it cost a lot? You see I haven't very much money.

MRS BROWN   Of course not. We wouldn't dream of charging you anything. We shall expect you to be one of the family, shan't we Henry.

MR BROWN   Of course. By the way, if you *are* coming home with us you'd better know our names. This is Mrs Brown and I'm Mr Brown.

PADDINGTON   [*raises his hat twice*] I haven't really got a name, only a Peruvian one which no one can understand.

MRS BROWN   Then we'd better give you an English one. It'll make things much easier. [*Thinking hard*] It ought to be something special. Now what shall we call you? I know! We found you on Paddington Station so that's what we'll call you . . . Paddington.

PADDINGTON   [*savouring it*] Paddington. Pad-ding-ton. Paddington. It seems a very long name.

MR BROWN   It's quite distinguished. Yes, I like Paddington as a name. Paddington it shall be.

MRS BROWN   Good. Now, Paddington, I have to meet our young daughter Judy off the train. I'm sure you must be thirsty after your long journey, so while I'm away Mr Brown will get you something to drink.

PADDINGTON Thank you.

MRS BROWN And for goodness sake, Henry, when you get a moment, take that label off his neck. It makes him look like a parcel.

[PADDINGTON *doesn't much like the thought of looking like a parcel*]

I'm sure he'll get put in a luggage van if a porter sees him. [*She goes off almost bumping into a* MAN *pushing the refreshment trolley*]

MR BROWN [*removing the label*] There we are. Ah! The very thing. Now I can get you something to drink.

[PADDINGTON *puts the luggage label into his suitcase*]

MAN What would you like, tea or coffee?

PADDINGTON Cocoa, please.

MAN [*annoyed*] We haven't got any cocoa.

PADDINGTON But you asked me what I would like . . .

MAN I asked you what would you like, *tea* or *coffee*!

MR BROWN [*hastily, trying to avoid an argument*] Perhaps you'd like a cold drink?

MAN Lemonade or orangeade?

PADDINGTON Marmalade.

MR BROWN [*before the man loses his temper*] I think some orangeade would be a good idea – and a cup of tea for me, please.

[*The* MAN *serves them*]

And perhaps you'd like a cake, Paddington?

PADDINGTON Oooh, yes, please.

MAN                Cream-and-chocolate, or cream-and-jam?

PADDINGTON   Yes, please.

MAN                Well, which do you want?

MR BROWN      We'd better have one of each.

[*The* MAN *puts them on a plate.* MR BROWN *pays him, and hands the plate to* PADDINGTON]

How's that to be going on with?

PADDINGTON   It's very nice, thank you, Mr Brown. But it's not very easy drinking out of a beaker. I usually get my nose stuck.

MR BROWN      Perhaps you'd like a straw. [*He takes one from the* MAN *and puts it into Paddington's beaker*]

PADDINGTON   That's a good idea. [*He blows through the straw and makes a noisy bubbling sound*] I'm glad I emigrated. [*Takes a bite from one of the cakes*] I wonder what else there is?

[*He puts the plate of cakes on the floor in order to peer at the trolley and promptly steps on the cake. In his excitement he upsets the rest of the cups on the trolley, scattering them in all directions. Trying to steady himself, he knocks Mr Brown's tea out of his hand, slips over and ends up sprawled on the platform. As* MR BROWN *bends to help him up* PADDINGTON *staggers to his feet. They collide and* PADDINGTON's *cream cake ends up plastered all over* MR BROWN's *face. Just at this moment* MRS BROWN *returns with* JUDY. *All this will need to be carefully rehearsed beforehand*]

MRS BROWN     Henry! Henry, whatever are you doing to that poor bear? Look at him! He's covered all over with jam and cream.

MR BROWN    *He's* covered with jam and cream! What about me? [*He begins to tidy up the mess*]

MRS BROWN    This is what happens when I leave your father alone for five minutes.

JUDY    [*clapping her hands*] Oh, Daddy, is he really going to stay with us?

[PADDINGTON *stands up, raises his hat, steps on the cake and falls over again*]

Oh, Mummy, isn't he funny!

MRS BROWN    You wouldn't think that anybody could get in such a state with just one cake.

MR BROWN    Perhaps we'd better go. Are we all ready?

JUDY    Come along, Paddington.

[PADDINGTON *picks up his suitcase and puts the remains of the cakes in it. The cake wrapper sticks to his paws but he doesn't notice it*]

We'll go straight home and you can have a nice hot bath. Then you can tell me all about South America. I'm sure you must have had lots of wonderful adventures.

PADDINGTON    I have. Lots. Things are always happening to me, I'm that sort of bear. [*He goes off with* JUDY]

MR BROWN    [*to his wife*] I hope we haven't bitten off more than we can chew.

MAN    Well, if you have, you'll just have to grin and *bear* it. [*He laughs loudly at his own joke and goes off* ]

# Scene Two

[*Number thirty-two, Windsor Gardens.* JUDY *and* PAD-
DINGTON *have just walked into the living room*]

JUDY          Here we are. Now you are going to meet
Mrs Bird.

PADDINGTON Mrs Bird?

JUDY          Yes. She looks after us. She's a bit fierce
sometimes and she grumbles a bit, but she
doesn't really mean it. I'm sure you'll like
her.

PADDINGTON [*nervously*] I'm sure I shall, if you say so.

[*The door opens and* MRS BIRD *appears*]

MRS BIRD      Goodness gracious, you've arrived already,
and me hardly finished the washing up. I
suppose you'll be wanting tea?

JUDY          Hello, Mrs Bird. It's nice to see you again.
How's the rheumatism?

MRS BIRD      Worse than it's ever been. [*She stops abruptly
as she sees* PADDINGTON] Good gracious!
Whatever have you got there?

JUDY          It's not a what, Mrs Bird. It's a bear. His
name's Paddington.

[PADDINGTON *raises his hat*]

MRS BIRD      A bear . . . well, he has good manners, I'll
say that for him.

JUDY          He's going to stay with us. He's come all
the way from South America and he's all
alone with nowhere to go.

MRS BIRD      Going to *stay* with us? How long for?

23

JUDY          I don't know. I suppose it *depends*!

MRS BIRD     Mercy me. I wish you'd told me he was coming. I haven't put clean sheets in the spare room or anything.

PADDINGTON It's all right, Mrs Bird. I didn't have any sheets in the lifeboat. I'm sure I shall be very comfortable.

[*He shakes hands with her. When he lets go, the leftover cake wrapper is sticking to her hand. She tries in vain to get it off, and finally it sticks to her other hand*]

JUDY          Let me help, Mrs Bird. [JUDY *takes it from her, but then finds that it is glued to her own hand*]

[*At this moment* MR *and* MRS BROWN *arrive with* JONATHAN]

                Hello, Jonathan. [*She shakes hands with* JONATHAN *and passes the sticky paper on to him*] You haven't met Paddington yet, have you? Paddington, this is my brother Jonathan.

JONATHAN   How do you do?

PADDINGTON Very well, thank you.

[PADDINGTON *shakes hands with* JONATHAN *and collects the sticky paper*]

MRS BIRD     Whatever's going on?

PADDINGTON I'm afraid I had an accident with a cake, Mrs Bird. It's left me a bit sticky.

MRS BIRD     I think a good hot bath will do you the world of good.

JUDY     [*confidentially*] She doesn't mind really. In fact, I think she rather likes you.

PADDINGTON  She seems a bit fierce.

MRS BIRD   [*turning round suddenly*] What was that?

PADDINGTON  I didn't hear anything.

MRS BIRD   Where was it you said you'd come from? Peru?

PADDINGTON  That's right. *Darkest* Peru.

MRS BIRD   Humph. Then I expect you like marmalade. I'd better get some more from the grocer. [*She leaves the room*]

JUDY     [*happily*] There you are! What did I tell you? She *does* like you.

PADDINGTON  Fancy her knowing that I like marmalade.

JUDY     Mrs Bird knows everything about everything.

MRS BROWN   Now, Judy, you'd better show Paddington his room.

JUDY     Come on. It used to be mine when I was small. There's a bathroom as well so you can have a good clean up.

PADDINGTON  A *bathroom*. Fancy having a special room for a bath.

[*They leave the room*]

MR BROWN   I hope we're doing the right thing.

MRS BROWN   Well, we can hardly turn him out now. It wouldn't be fair.

MR BROWN     I'm sure we ought to report the matter to
             someone first.

JONATHAN     I don't see why, Dad. Besides, didn't you
             say he was a stowaway? He might get
             arrested.

MR BROWN     Then there's the question of pocket money.
             I'm not sure how much money to give a
             bear.

MRS BROWN    He can have twenty pence a week, the same
             as Jonathan and Judy.

MR BROWN     Very well, but we'll have to see what Mrs
             Bird has to say about it first.

JONATHAN     Hurrah!

MRS BROWN    *You'd* better ask her then, it was your idea.

[MRS BIRD *comes in with a tray of tea, followed by* JUDY]

MRS BIRD     I suppose you want to tell me you've
             decided to keep that young Paddington.

JUDY         May we, Mrs Bird? *Please.* I'm sure he'll
             be very good.

MRS BIRD     Humph! [*She puts the tray on the table*] That
             remains to be seen. Different people have
             different ideas about being good. All the
             same, he looks the sort of bear who means
             well.

MR BROWN     Then you don't mind, Mrs Bird?

MRS BIRD     No. No, I don't mind at all. I've always had
             a soft spot for bears myself. It'll be nice to
             have one about the house. [*She goes*]

MR BROWN     Well, whoever would have thought it?

JUDY    I expect it was because he raised his hat. It made a good impression.

MRS BROWN    [*pouring the tea*] I suppose someone ought to write and tell his Aunt Lucy. I'm sure she'd like to know how he's getting on.

MR BROWN    By the way, how *is* he getting on?

[*There is a loud gurgling noise from the bath, followed by a tremendous splashing sound.* PADDINGTON *begins to sing*]

JUDY    Oh, all right, I think. At least, he seemed all right when I left him.

[MR BROWN *suddenly feels his head*]

MR BROWN    That's funny. I could have sworn I felt a spot of water.

MRS BROWN    Don't be silly, Henry. How could you?

MR BROWN    [*another drop lands on his head*] It's happened again!

JONATHAN    [*looks up at the ceiling*] Crikey! [*He nudges* JUDY] Look!

JUDY    [*looks up too*] Oh, gosh! The bath!

JONATHAN    Come on!

MR BROWN    Where are you two going?

JUDY    Oh . . . [*pretending to be casual*] We're just going upstairs to see how Paddington's getting on. [*She bundles* JONATHAN *out of the room*] Quick!

MRS BROWN    What was all that about, I wonder?

MR BROWN    I don't know, Mary. I suppose they're just excited about having a bear in the house . . .

JUDY            [*calls offstage*] Are you all right, Paddington?

PADDINGTON  Yes, I think so.

JUDY            Gosh! Look at the mess.

JONATHAN   Why on earth didn't you turn the tap off?
No wonder all the water overflowed.

PADDINGTON  I'm afraid I got soap in my eyes. I couldn't
see anything.

[*As he is led back into the room by* JONATHAN *and*
JUDY, *he squeezes water out of his hat*]

It's a good thing I had my hat with me. I
used it to bail the water out. I might have
drowned otherwise.

MR BROWN   No wonder I thought I felt some water.

JUDY            Now you just dry yourself properly, or
you'll catch cold. [*She drapes a towel round
him*]

PADDINGTON  [*proudly as he looks at himself*] I'm a lot
cleaner than I was.

[MRS BIRD *enters*]

MRS BIRD    You'd better give me your hat, Paddington.
I'll put it on the line.

PADDINGTON  [*puts his hat back on*] I'd rather you didn't,
Mrs Bird. I don't like being without it. It's
my special bush hat and it belonged to my
uncle.

MRS BROWN  In that case, perhaps you'd like to tell us all
about yourself, and how you came to
emigrate.

PADDINGTON  [*sits down in an armchair and makes the most of*

*his audience*] Well . . . I was brought up by
my Aunt Lucy. [*He closes his eyes*]

JONATHAN        Your Aunt Lucy?

PADDINGTON    [*sleepily*] Yes. She's the one who lives in the
Home for Retired Bears in [SNORE]-ima . . .

MR BROWN       [*puzzled*] In [SNORE]-ima! Where's that?

PADDINGTON    It's in Peru, Mr Brown. [SNORE] *Darkest
Peru.*

JUDY                  Paddington . . . wake up.

[PADDINGTON *gives a longer snore.* MR BROWN *pokes
him gently*]

MR BROWN       Well I never. I do believe he's fallen asleep.

MRS BROWN      [*drapes the towel round him to make him more
comfortable*] I'm not really surprised. I don't
suppose there are many bears who've had
quite such a busy day!

JONATHAN
JUDY                  [*in chorus*] Especially from [SNORE]-ima.

## CURTAIN

# Paddington Paints a Picture

# CAST OF CHARACTERS

MR BROWN

PADDINGTON

MR GRUBER

MRS BIRD

MISS BLACK

JONATHAN

JUDY

MAN

# PROPS

*In the Browns' sitting room:*
A few chairs
Table
Easel

(for scenes III and IV):
Very messy painting
Paint brush
Paints – red and green
Marmalade jar
Spoon
Palette (can be made from cardboard)
Three empty bottles, painted to look as
if they contain paint remover, ketchup
and mustard
Handkerchief
Washing-up liquid
Slip of paper for cheque
*In Mr Gruber's shop:*
Chair
Sign saying "Antiques"
Thermos flask, two mugs and a bun
Pile of bric-a-brac, china, books, toys
*Half-restored "painting"

In this play the easel with Mr Brown's painting should be placed near the centre of the stage so that Paddington has plenty of room to work on it. We don't need to see the painting, as it will be facing away from us until Miss Black brings it back at the end of the play. Of course, the tomato ketchup and mustard and paint remover should not be real (use empty bottles painted to look full), and the painting should be done beforehand so that it is dry for the performance. The painting should look as messy as you can make it.

When we get to Mr Gruber's shop, all that we need to see is a pile of oddments with a notice saying "Antiques". Mr Gruber should have a chair to sit on, *a half-cleaned picture with a boat on one side and part of a lady's face on the other, a thermos flask and two mugs.

# Scene One

[*The Browns' sitting room.* MR BROWN *is getting ready to go to work as* PADDINGTON *comes in. The easel is standing with its back to the audience*]

MR BROWN      Hello, Paddington, what are your plans for today?

PADDINGTON    I think I might do some shopping, Mr Brown. I like shopping.

MR BROWN      You won't get lost?

PADDINGTON    No, I won't be going very far. Is your painting finished, Mr Brown?

MR BROWN      Yes. [*He looks at it*] You know, I really think it's the best I've ever done.

PADDINGTON    I hope you win a prize.

MR BROWN      Oh, I don't expect I shall. But it's fun, that's the important thing, I suppose. I must be off now, I'm late for work already. [*He goes to the door*] Goodbye, Paddington. I'll see you tonight.

PADDINGTON    Goodbye, Mr Brown.

[MR BROWN *goes, and* PADDINGTON *takes a closer look at the painting*]

I think I would enjoy painting. It looks *very* interesting.

# Scene Two

[*Mr Gruber's bric-a-brac shop in the Portobello Road. He is cleaning an oil painting when* PADDINGTON *arrives*]

MR GRUBER     Good morning. Can I help you?

PADDINGTON    [*putting down his suitcase*] I don't know really. I was out for a walk and your shop looked so nice, I thought I would like to see inside.

MR GRUBER    Please have a look round, Mr . . . er . . .

PADDINGTON    Brown. Paddington Brown. I come from Darkest Peru.

MR GRUBER    Darkest Peru? How strange. I know Peru quite well. I spent a lot of my early life in South America.

PADDINGTON    Fancy that, Mr . . . er . . .

MR GRUBER    Gruber. Look . . . I've just made some cocoa, Mr Brown. Would you care for a cup?

PADDINGTON    Ooh, yes, please.

MR GRUBER    It's quite hot. I keep it in a vacuum.

PADDINGTON    [*amazed*] You keep your cocoa in a vacuum cleaner?

MR GRUBER    No, Mr Brown, a vacuum flask. [*He pours some cocoa and hands it to* PADDINGTON] There's nothing like a chat over a bun and a cup of cocoa.

PADDINGTON    A bun as well! [*They sit down to enjoy their elevenses*] What were you doing when I came into the shop, Mr Gruber?

MR GRUBER    I was cleaning a painting. [*He picks it up*] Now, what do you think of that?

PADDINGTON    [*looking at it*] It's a puzzle, Mr Gruber. One half is a boat and the other half is a lady in a large hat.

MR GRUBER     There you are. I'd like your opinion on it, Mr Brown.

PADDINGTON    It doesn't seem to be one thing or the other.

MR GRUBER     Ah! It isn't at the moment. But just you wait until I've cleaned it! I gave five shillings for that painting years and years ago, when it was just a picture of a sailing ship. And what do you think? When I started to clean it the other day, all the paint began to come off and I discovered that there was another painting underneath. [*Confidentially*] It could be an old master.

PADDINGTON    An old master? It looks like an old lady to me.

MR GRUBER     [*laughs*] What I mean is, it could be very valuable. It could be by a famous painter.

PADDINGTON    That sounds interesting. Very interesting indeed. [*He gets up, his mind obviously elsewhere*] I'll have to be going now, Mr Gruber. Thank you for the elevenses.

MR GRUBER     Is anything the matter, Mr Brown?

PADDINGTON    No, Mr Gruber. I've had an idea, that's all. [*Mysteriously, as he makes to leave*] I may come into some money soon.

MR GRUBER     Good day, Mr Brown. I shall look forward to that. [*He watches* PADDINGTON *go*] Come into some money! I wonder what he meant by that?

# Scene Three

[*The Browns' sitting room.* PADDINGTON *comes in, looks round carefully. He takes a bottle of paint remover from his coat pocket. He soaks a handkerchief in paint remover and rubs it over the painting. He stands back to look, and horrified by what he sees, decides to have another try. He is giving the painting a vigorous scrub when* MRS BIRD *enters*]

MRS BIRD     Now, Paddington, what are you up to? I thought you were out shopping.

PADDINGTON     I was. But I'm not any more. [*Gloomily*] I wish I still was.

MRS BIRD     Whatever's the matter? [*She sees the picture*] What *have* you been doing? That's the painting Mr Brown did specially for the exhibition.

PADDINGTON     I know. I thought there might be an old master underneath.

MRS BIRD     An old master? [*She looks at the painting*] It used to be some boats on a lake. It looks more like a storm at sea now. He'll be most upset when he sees it.

PADDINGTON     I know, Mrs Bird, what can I do?

MRS BIRD     They're coming to collect it today. There's only one hope, perhaps you could touch it up before they get here.

PADDINGTON     That's a good idea, Mrs Bird. Except I haven't any paints.

MRS BIRD     There's an old box under the stairs. I'll get them for you. [*She goes*]

PADDINGTON   I wonder if it will work. [*He gets a jar of marmalade, takes a spoonful, and then puts it on the table near the easel*]

MRS BIRD   [*coming in with a paintbox and palette*] Here we are. It's very old, but it's the best I can do.

PADDINGTON   Thank you, Mrs Bird.

MRS BIRD   I hope you manage something. I don't know I'm sure . . . [*She goes to the kitchen*]

PADDINGTON   [*holding the brush at arm's length, he considers the canvas*] Uh, huh. [*He squeezes a tube of red paint on the palette, then he does the same with a green tube. He begins to paint boldly. Although we can't see the painting, it is obvious that he is making a mess*] That looks better! [*Throughout this painting scene* PADDINGTON *occasionally touches the brush to his face, without realizing he is giving himself red and green spots. He dabs at the painting, absent-mindedly dipping his brush into the marmalade, and then decides to experiment. First he adds some mustard, and then the contents of a washing-up liquid squeezer and a bottle of tomato ketchup*] There's one thing about painting, it's fun. [*He makes a huge mess of it.* MISS BLACK *arrives to collect the picture and knocks at the front door.* PADDINGTON *puts down his brush and goes to the door*]

MISS BLACK   Good afternoon. I believe Mr Brown has a painting for our exhibition.

PADDINGTON    Oh, yes. That's right. I'll get it for you. [*He goes back, gives the painting a finishing dab, wipes the brush on his hat, and takes the painting to the front door*]

MISS BLACK    Thank you very much. The final judging takes place this afternoon.

PADDINGTON    The *final* judging?

MISS BLACK    Yes, we shall be awarding the prizes today. I expect you will hear the results later this evening. Goodbye. [*She goes*]

PADDINGTON    Goodbye. There's something else about painting – it's fun while it lasts, but it's much more difficult than it looks. I can't think what Mr Brown will say . . .

## Scene Four

[*Later that day. The* BROWN *family are in the sitting room after dinner*]

MRS BROWN    Would you like a cup of cocoa, Paddington?

PADDINGTON    No, thank you.

MRS BROWN    Are you all right?

PADDINGTON    Yes, I thank so, think you. I mean, I think so, thank you.

MRS BROWN    Nothing on your mind?

PADDINGTON    No.

JONATHAN    How about a bull's-eye?

PADDINGTON    No, thank you. I think I'll just go and have a rest for a bit. [*He goes out of the room*]

MRS BROWN   I do hope he's all right, Henry. He hardly touched his dinner, and that's not like him at all. And he seemed to have some funny red spots all over his face.

JONATHAN   Red spots! I wonder if it's measles. I hope he's given it to me, whatever it is. Then I will be able to stay away from school.

JUDY   Well, he's got green ones as well. I distinctly saw them.

MR BROWN   Green ones! I wonder if he's sickening for something? If they're not gone in the morning, we'd better send for the doctor.

JONATHAN   They're judging the paintings today, aren't they, Dad?

MR BROWN   Yes, they took mine away this afternoon.

JONATHAN   Do you think you'll win a prize?

MRS BROWN   No one will be more surprised than your father if he does. He's never won a prize yet.

MR BROWN   It took me a long while but I don't suppose I'll be any luckier than last time. The lady who collected it this afternoon told Paddington that the results would be made known today, so we'll soon know.

JUDY   I wonder if he's feeling any better? [*She goes out*]

JONATHAN   Perhaps they have *green* measles in Darkest Peru.

[*There is a knock at the front door.* MRS BIRD *goes to answer it*]

| | |
|---|---|
| MRS BIRD | Who can that be? |

[MRS BIRD *opens the door.* MISS BLACK *is waiting outside. She has a* MAN *with her. He is carrying Mr Brown's painting, still with its back to the audience*]

| | |
|---|---|
| MISS BLACK | Good evening. Is Mr Brown in? |
| MAN | We've come about the painting he entered for our competition. |
| MRS BIRD | Oh, dear. Will you come this way, please? |
| | [*She ushers them into the room*] |
| MAN | Mr Brown? |
| MR BROWN | That's right. |
| MAN | I'm the President of the Art Society, and this is Miss Black, who was one of the judges of the competition. |
| MR BROWN | How do you do. |
| MAN | I've some news for you, Mr Brown. |
| PADDINGTON | [*offstage*] Oooooh! |
| MISS BLACK | Good gracious! What was that? |
| MAN | It sounded like a cow mooing somewhere. |
| MRS BROWN | I think it's only a bear oooohing. |
| MAN | Oh! Er . . . Mr Brown, as I was saying, the judges decided that your painting was most unusual . . . |
| MRS BIRD | It certainly was. |
| MAN | And they have all agreed to award you the first prize. |
| MR BROWN | The *first* prize? |
| MISS BLACK | Yes, they thought your painting showed great imagination. |

41

| | |
|---|---|
| MR BROWN | [*pleased*] Did they now? |
| MAN | It made great use of marmalade chunks. |
| THE BROWNS | [*chorus*] Marmalade chunks! |
| MAN | Yes, indeed. I don't think I've ever come across anything quite like it before [*He places the painting on the easel facing the audience. It is, to say the least, unusual, and there are several real marmalade chunks sticking to it*] |
| MRS BROWN | I didn't know you were interested in abstract art, Henry. |
| MR BROWN | Nor did I! |

[PADDINGTON *and* JUDY *put their heads round the door*]

| | |
|---|---|
| MAN | [*he removes a marmalade chunk with a flourish and swallows it*] It not only looks good – it tastes good! |
| MISS BLACK | What are you calling it? |
| MR BROWN | Where's Paddington? |
| MISS BLACK | Where's Paddington? What a funny title! |
| MAN | Well, sir, my congratulations! We'll be wanting the painting back in a day or so to put into the exhibition, but I'll leave it with you for the moment. Just one more thing . . . your prize. [*He hands over a cheque*] £10. |
| MISS BLACK | May I ask what you will do with it, Mr Brown? |
| MR BROWN | [*wearily*] I think perhaps I'd better give it to a certain Home for Retired Bears in South America. |

MAN          Oh, really? Well, we must be getting along.
      [*As they leave* PADDINGTON *falls into the room.* JUDY
      *follows him in*]

MRS BIRD     Well, Paddington. The secret's out. Now,
             what have you got to say for yourself?

PADDINGTON   [*crosses to the painting. He removes a marma-
             lade chunk and goes to eat it*] I think it looks
             good enough to eat, Mr Brown! [*He
             turns it up the other way*] But I think they
             might have put it the right way up. After
             all, it's not every day a bear wins first prize
             in a painting competition.

   CURTAIN

# Paddington Has a Birthday

# CAST OF CHARACTERS

MR GRUBER

PADDINGTON

MRS BROWN

MRS BIRD

JUDY

JONATHAN

MR CURRY

MR BROWN

## PROPS

*In Mr Gruber's shop:*
Piles of bric-a-brac
Two chairs
Candlestick
Two mugs
Cardboard box (the conjuring set) and "magic wand"
Small table
Paddington's suitcase and marmalade jar
*Long cloth
Small cloth
Book

*In the Browns' sitting room*
Chairs and table
Cake (not necessarily a real cake)
Candle
Matches
Plates
*Egg
Small packet (Paddington's sandwich)
*Toy watch
Toy rubber hammer

Mr Gruber's shop is just as we saw it in the last play. The conjuring set is simple to make: you will need a short rod to use as a wand and a small table covered by a *long cloth, with a pocket hanging down at the back. PADDINGTON will need to practise making the egg disappear and producing the marmalade with the help of the pocket.

*For the egg, use a broken eggshell that has been glued or sellotaped together.

*Mr Curry's watch can be made using a wide rubber band for the strap and a milkbottle top for the face.

# Scene One

[*Mr Gruber's shop in the Portobello Road.* MR GRUBER *is polishing an old candlestick when* PADDINGTON *arrives. He is carrying his suitcase containing a jar of marmalade*]

MR GRUBER   Good morning, Mr Brown.

PADDINGTON   Good morning, Mr Gruber.

MR GRUBER   You've chosen a good time to call.

PADDINGTON   Have I?

MR GRUBER   Yes, it's just eleven o'clock. Time for buns and cocoa.

PADDINGTON   So it is! But I really came to ask you something. Mr Gruber, do you like parties?

MR GRUBER   Yes, I do, Mr Brown. I don't get invited to many nowadays, but I always enjoy them when I do.

PADDINGTON   Would you like to come to *my* party on Monday?

MR GRUBER   I'd be delighted. Is it your birthday?

PADDINGTON   Yes, it's my summer one.

MR GRUBER   Your summer one?

PADDINGTON   I have one in the winter as well. Bears have two birthdays every year, like the Queen.

MR GRUBER   I see. Well, I'll look forward to it very much indeed, Mr Brown. What time shall I come?

PADDINGTON   About four o'clock.

MR GRUBER   Right. I've got something in here which might come in useful. It isn't brand new, but it's very unusual. [*He brings a cardboard box from the back of the shop*] It's a conjuring set.

PADDINGTON    A conjuring set!

MR GRUBER    If you take it home with you today you'll have a chance to practise some of the tricks before Monday. Then you can entertain everybody at the party.

PADDINGTON    What a good idea. Thank you very much, Mr Gruber.

MR GRUBER    [*he opens the box*] There's a magic wand and a magic table which will help you to make things disappear. [*He sets it up*] Could you lend me your marmalade for a moment, Mr Brown?

PADDINGTON    [*looking in his case*] Here you are, Mr Gruber. There isn't very much left, I'm afraid. [*He hands the jar to* MR GRUBER]

MR GRUBER    That will do very well. [*He places the jar on the table and covers it with a cloth*] Now, I wave the wand thus and say the magic word Abracadabra! [*He lifts the cloth and the marmalade has disappeared – into the pocket in the cloth*]

PADDINGTON    [*amazed*] It's disappeared!

MR GRUBER    Exactly. [*He hands the wand to* PADDINGTON] Now, I'll just hold the cloth here, and if you say the magic word . . .

PADDINGTON    Marmalade!

MR GRUBER    No, not that! Abracadabra!

PADDINGTON    Abracadabra!

MR GRUBER    [*he lifts the cloth*] There we are . . . safely back again. [*He returns the jar of marmalade to* PADDINGTON]

49

PADDINGTON That's very clever. How do you do it?

MR GRUBER It's quite easy really. There's a secret compartment under the table, and the marmalade dropped into it while I was holding the cloth.

PADDINGTON Are there some more tricks in the box, Mr Gruber?

MR GRUBER Oh, yes, quite a lot. And there's a book of instructions. But you must follow them very carefully.

PADDINGTON Thank you very much, Mr Gruber. And thank you for the cocoa. I'll see you on Monday. [*He goes, taking the box with him*]

MR GRUBER Good day, Mr Brown. Don't forget, read the instructions carefully!

## Scene Two

[*The Browns' sitting room.* MRS BIRD *is laying the table*]

MRS BROWN Is everything ready, Mrs Bird?

MRS BIRD Yes. [*Putting the candle on the cake*] Now, how many will there be? You and Mr Brown, Jonathan, Judy, and Paddington – that's five, then Mr Gruber and me, that's seven.

MRS BROWN And Mr Curry.

MRS BIRD Mr Curry! I didn't know he'd been invited.

MRS BROWN He wasn't. He invited himself.

MRS BIRD Just because there's a free tea. I expect he'll even complain about that. I think it's

disgusting, taking the crumbs off a young
bear's plate like that.

MRS BROWN   He'll have to look slippy if he expects to
get any crumbs off Paddington's plate.

JUDY   [*coming in*] Fancy! He lives next door and
he didn't even bother to wish Paddington
many happy returns!

MRS BROWN   Perhaps he will when the party starts.

JONATHAN   [*coming in*] It's four o'clock, isn't anybody
here yet?

[*A knock at the door as* MR GRUBER *arrives, closely
followed by* MR CURRY]

MRS BROWN   There's somebody now.

PADDINGTON   It's all right, Mrs Bird, I'll go. [*He goes to
let* MR GRUBER *in*] Hello, Mr Gruber.
Hello, Mr Curry. Please come in.

MR GRUBER   Thank you, Mr Brown.

MR CURRY   Thank you, bear.

MRS BROWN   Hello, it's very kind of you both to come.

JONATHAN   Where's Dad?

MR BROWN   [*appearing from the kitchen*] Here I am. Hello,
Mr Gruber. Good afternoon, Mr Curry.

MR GRUBER   Good afternoon.

MR BROWN   Well now, we all know why we're here.

PADDINGTON   Yes!

MR BROWN   Because it's Paddington's birthday.

JONATHAN   Hurrah!

[PADDINGTON *goes outside*]

51

MR BROWN        And now, before we light the candle and get down to the real business of the afternoon . . . I think Paddington has a surprise for us. He's going to do some conjuring.

[PADDINGTON *returns, carrying the conjuror's table, wand, and his book of instructions*]

PADDINGTON      [*waving his wand for silence, after looking at his instruction book*) Ladies and gentlemen, my next trick is impossible.

MR CURRY        Your *next* trick, but you haven't done one yet!

PADDINGTON      [*ignoring the interruption*] For this trick I shall require an egg.

MRS BIRD        Oh dear! [*She goes off to get one*]

MRS BROWN       I feel sure something dreadful is going to happen.

JONATHAN        I wonder if he's got a rabbit inside his hat.

PADDINGTON      [*raises his hat and a small parcel falls out*] I don't think so. Only some marmalade sandwiches.

MRS BIRD        [*returns with a dummy egg*] Here you are, Paddington.

PADDINGTON      [*taking it with a slight bow*] Thank you, Mrs Bird. I now place the egg in the centre of my magic table and cover it with the cloth, so. [*To* JONATHAN] Now, sir, you're quite sure the egg is there?

JONATHAN        Absolutely sure.

PADDINGTON      Good. [*He waves his wand*] Abracadabra! [*He lifts the cloth and the egg has disappeared into the pocket at the back of the table*]

JONATHAN      That's very good!

JUDY          I wonder how he does it.

MR CURRY      It's quite easy really. It's all done by sleight of paw. Not bad though, for a bear. But can you bring it back again?

PADDINGTON    [*putting the cloth back over the table*] Abracadabra! Now, ladies and gentlemen, when I lift the cloth, you will see that the egg has returned. [*He whisks away the cloth and is surprised to find a jar of marmalade instead*] That's funny!

MR CURRY      Oh, yes. Very funny. Making us think you were going to find an egg and it was a jar of marmalade all the time!

MR GRUBER     Very good, Mr Brown. [*They all clap*]

PADDINGTON    [*after taking a bow*] Thank you. For my next trick I need a watch.

MR BROWN      [*anxiously*] Are you sure? Wouldn't anything else do?

PADDINGTON    [*consulting the book*] It says a watch.

MR CURRY      Here you are, bear, I'll lend you mine. Only it's very valuable, so look after it.

PADDINGTON    Thank you, Mr Curry. [*He places it on the table*] This is a very good trick. [*He covers the watch with the cloth*] Now, I take this hammer [*He takes a hammer from the box*] and I hit the watch with it, so! [*He hammers the watch*]

MR CURRY      [*rising*] I hope you know what you're doing, young bear.

PADDINGTON [*he hits it again*] Now, Mr Curry, perhaps you'll lift the cloth for me. [MR CURRY *lifts the cloth and sees his battered watch*]

MR CURRY What's this?

PADDINGTON Oh, dear! I think I forgot to say abracadabra.

MR CURRY Abracadabra! *Abracadabra!* [*He snatches up the remains of the watch*] Twenty years I've had this watch, and now look at it. Shockproof . . .

MR BROWN It doesn't look very shock-proof to me.

MR CURRY Seventeen jewels!

PADDINGTON [*he pretends to sweep up some remains and hands them to* MR CURRY] There are still some left, Mr Curry.

MR CURRY Pah!

MR GRUBER May I see that watch a moment? [*He examines it carefully*]

MR CURRY You may – what's left of it!

MR GRUBER There may not be much left, Mr Curry, but I know one of my own watches when I see it. You bought this from me for fifty pence not six months ago! You ought to be ashamed of yourself, telling lies like that in front of a young bear.

MR CURRY Rubbish! [He *sits down grumpily in the armchair and is horrified when he realizes that something very unpleasant has happened*] I'm sitting on something wet and sticky!

PADDINGTON    Oh dear, I expect it's my disappearing egg. It must have reappeared.

MR CURRY    [*rising furiously*] I've never been so insulted in my life. Never! [*He points an accusing finger at the company*] It's the last time I shall ever come to one of *your* birthday parties. [*He storms out*]

MRS BROWN    [*as* MR BROWN *begins to laugh*] Henry, you really oughtn't to laugh.

MR BROWN    It's no good, I can't help it.

MR GRUBER    [*joining in*] Did you see his face when all of the cogs fell out?

JONATHAN    And when Paddington gave him back his jewels?

JUDY    [*imitating Paddington*] There are still some left, Mr Curry. [*By this time they are helpless with laughter*]

MR GRUBER    I bet the man who invented that trick never saw it performed better.

PADDINGTON    I'm glad you enjoyed it. Would you like me to do some more?

MR BROWN    [*hastily*] No, thank you. The secret of success as an entertainer is to leave the audience wanting more.

MRS BIRD    [*lighting the candle*] I suggest we see if we can make that cake disappear instead.

JUDY    Now, Paddington, you must blow out the candle and make a wish.

PADDINGTON    I wish . . .

JONATHAN    No, you mustn't tell your wish to anybody.

PADDINGTON   All right. I wish [*He thinks a wish*] I wish . . .
             [*He blows out the candle*]

MR GRUBER    Happy Birthday, Mr Brown. [*They all
             cheer*]

PADDINGTON   Yes, it is. A very happy birthday.

JONATHAN     I've an idea. Let's all sing Happy Birthday.
             Are you ready?

ALL          Yes.

JONATHAN     Here we go then.

ALL          Happy Birthday to you,
             Happy Birthday to you,
             Happy Birthday dear Paddington,
             Happy Birthday to you.

   [*They cheer as the play ends*]

# CURTAIN

# Paddington Visits the Dentist

# CAST OF CHARACTERS

MRS BROWN
MR BROWN
JUDY
JONATHAN
MRS BIRD
PADDINGTON
MR LEACH, the dentist
NURSE

## PROPS

*At the Browns' house:*
Chairs and table
Plates

*At the dentist's surgery:*
Chair
Table
Scarf
Glass of orange squash
Tray for dentist's instruments
Metal ballpoint pen for syringe
*Toy false teeth
Large piece of chewing gum or soft sweet
Paper bag of sweets
Small brush
Two white coats

The Browns' dining room at Number thirty-two, Windsor Gardens is not very different from their sitting room. A table and chairs are all that is necessary. For Mr Leach's surgery we will require a chair for PADDINGTON to sit in when his teeth are examined, a beaker of orange squash (in place of mouthwash), a small metal ballpoint pen (for the syringe) and a model of *Mr Leach's teeth stuck in toffee and concealed in his coat pocket before the play starts. These can be toy teeth or made from plasticine. MR LEACH and the NURSE should both wear white coats over their clothes.

# Scene One

[*The Browns' dining room. The Browns have just finished breakfast and* JUDY *and* JONATHAN *are helping to clear away.*]

MRS BROWN  We shall never hear the last of it. I'm sure of that.

MR BROWN  [*as he enters*] What's that, Mary?

MRS BROWN  Paddington's tooth. It's been put into the waste disposal unit by mistake.

JUDY  And he wanted to keep it to put under his pillow, so that he would find five pence in the morning. He's very upset.

MR BROWN  Well, he could try leaving a note under his pillow explaining what happened.

JUDY  Perhaps it would be worth looking under the drain cover. It might still be there.

JONATHAN  I shouldn't think so. Those waste disposals are very good. They grind up everything.

MRS BROWN  I don't think he's lost a tooth at all, I think he broke a piece off when he was testing his everlasting toffee.

MR BROWN  Whatever is everlasting toffee?

MRS BIRD  You may well ask. It's something Paddington invented yesterday. It set so hard it took me two hours to get it off the saucepan.

PADDINGTON  [*offstage*] Ooooh!

MR BROWN  What are we going to do about him?

MRS BIRD  I've arranged an appointment with the dentist. Mr Leach is seeing him this morning.

PADDINGTON [*enters*] Ooooh!

MR BROWN  I'm sorry to hear you've lost your tooth, Paddington.

PADDINGTON  Yes. I've had it ever since I was born and I've cleaned it twice every day. I don't know what Aunt Lucy's going to say when I tell her.

MRS BROWN  Let's worry about that later. Mrs Bird has made an appointment with Mr Leach.

PADDINGTON  Mr Leach?

MRS BROWN  Our dentist. I'm sure he'll soon put you right. He's been practising for years.

PADDINGTON  Mr Leach has been *practising*? I think I'd sooner pay extra and have somebody who knows what he's doing . . .

## Scene Two

[*Mr Leach's surgery.* MR LEACH *is talking to his* NURSE]

MR LEACH  Who have we first today, Miss Kay?

NURSE  Mrs Brown, sir. An emergency appointment.

[*She goes through the surgery door and ushers in* MRS BROWN *and* PADDINGTON, *wearing a scarf tied round his head and under his chin*]

MR LEACH  Good morning, Mrs Brown.

MRS BROWN  Good morning, Mr Leach.

MR LEACH  Now, what can I do for you?

MRS BROWN  It's Paddington. He's having trouble with a tooth.

MR LEACH        Hmm. Well, I'm afraid I shall have to charge extra. Bears have forty-two teeth.

PADDINGTON  I've only got forty-one. One of mine's been disposed of.

MR LEACH        That's still nine more than I usually deal with. I shall have to get my nurse to draw up a completely new chart. Now, perhaps you'll sit yourself down there. [*He ushers* PADDINGTON *into the chair and then goes round the back.* PADDINGTON *jumps out of the chair and hurries round the back in order to see what's going on. As he does so,* MR LEACH *comes round the front*]

MR LEACH        Where is he? Nurse, what's happened to my patient?

NURSE           He was here a moment ago.

[*They both go round the back of the chair just as* PADDINGTON *comes round to the front again*]

PADDINGTON  [*settling down*] Here I am, Mr Leach. [*He removes his scarf, opens his mouth and points to it*] It's in here. At least, it was!

MR LEACH        I can see this is going to be one of those days. [*He examines Paddington's teeth, peering into his mouth*] Say aah!

PADDINGTON  Aaah . . .

MR LEACH        [*he feels a tooth with his finger*] Mmm. Mmmmmm. Uh, huh.

PADDINGTON  [*copying*] Mm. Mmmmmm. Uh, huh.

[*This can be repeated if it gets a laugh*]

MR LEACH        [*breathing heavily as he gives up*] I think that
                will be enough, thank you.

PADDINGTON      [*standing up*] Thank *you*, Mr Leach. That
                didn't hurt at all.

MR LEACH        I haven't done anything yet. That was only
                an inspection – just to see what's what.
                We've a long way to go yet, I'm afraid.
                You have what is known as a fractured
                cusp.

PADDINGTON      A fractured cusp! It was all right when I
                came in. You must have poked it with
                your finger.

MR LEACH        A fractured cusp simply means that you
                have a broken tooth. You have quite a
                large piece missing.

PADDINGTON      Oh, dear! I think I'd like a glass of orange-
                ade. [*He goes to drink the mouthwash*]

MR LEACH        That is *not* orangeade. It's put there for
                patients to use afterwards.

PADDINGTON      [*hands the beaker to the* NURSE] I'm very
                sorry, Patience, I didn't know it was yours.
                There's still some left.

NURSE           Thank you. [*Takes the beaker and starts to
                drink*]

MR LEACH        Nurse! [*He picks up the syringe*] Now, we're
                going to have something to take our mind
                off your tooth.

PADDINGTON      You mean, a bun?

MR LEACH        No, an injection. Open wide. [*He gives*
                PADDINGTON *the injection*] There! That
                didn't hurt, did it?

63

PADDINGTON  Not at all, thank you. [*He stands up and takes the syringe*] Shall I give you yours now?

MR LEACH  [*jumps back*] Mine! *I* don't have an injection.

PADDINGTON  But you said *we* were going to have something to take *our* mind off *my* tooth.

MR LEACH  Nurse! I think we'll try taking a wax impression. It may make things easier . . . and quieter.

NURSE  Yes, sir. [*She hands him a piece of "wax", which could be a large piece of chewing gum or other soft sweet*]

MR LEACH  Now, I want you to open your mouth again, say "ah" and when I've put this in, take a good, hard bite.

PADDINGTON  Aaaaah!

MR LEACH  Good. Now, one more "ah" like that. And whatever happens from now on – don't let go.

PADDINGTON  Aaaaah! [*He bites on the "wax", trapping Mr Leach's thumb*]

MR LEACH  Oooooooh!

PADDINGTON  Oooooooh!

MR LEACH  Owwwwwwwwwww!

PADDINGTON  Owwwwwwwwwww!

MR LEACH  Let go!

[PADDINGTON *shakes his head*]
Help, somebody!

MRS BROWN   Oh, dear. Nurse, you grab Mr Leach. I'll pull Paddington.

[*There is a tremendous tug of war. Finally* PADDINGTON *lets go and* MR LEACH *and the* NURSE *fall over*]

MR LEACH   Why didn't you let go?

PADDINGTON   You told me not to. You said bite hard and don't let go, whatever happens. [*He hands* MR LEACH *the* "*wax*"]

MR LEACH   [*examines it*] I wanted an impression of your teeth – not my thumb!

MRS BROWN   Mr Leach, would you like us to come back another day?

MR LEACH   [*bravely*] No. No, I'll just paint your tooth with this liquid to stop it from hurting. [*he does this*] And if you'll come back next week, I'll give you a nice, new, gold tooth to replace the one that's missing.

PADDINGTON   [*delighted*] A *gold* tooth! I shall keep it for Sundays . . . I shan't eat with it.

MR LEACH   Er . . . yes.

MRS BROWN   That sounds splendid.

PADDINGTON   Thank you very much, Mr Leach. It's very kind of you. [*He offers him a paper bag*] Perhaps you'd like to try one of these?

MR LEACH   I . . . er . . . I don't normally eat toffees. It doesn't set a very good example. But I must say they look rather tempting. [*He helps himself*] It's most kind of you. [*He chews on one of Paddington's everlasting toffees*] It's really very good . . . [*His jaws stick together*] Grrr! Glug!

PADDINGTON I'm glad you like it, Mr Leach. It's a new kind of toffee I've just invented. They're everlasting.

[MR LEACH *staggers about the surgery, trying to open his jaws. When he eventually succeeds, he pretends to remove a large lump of toffee from his mouth. There is what looks like a set of false teeth embedded in it. He holds it up for everybody to see and points to the teeth. From now on he has to pretend he has no teeth*]

MR LEACH My teeth! [*He collapses into the chair*] Look at them! [*He puts the teeth down on the instrument tray*]

PADDINGTON I think perhaps you've fractured your cusps, Mr Leach. If you open your mouth, I'll soon put it right for you. [*He picks up the syringe*]

MR LEACH [*opens his mouth and then realizes what he is doing*] Oh, no, you don't! [*He rushes out*]

PADDINGTON Oh, dear. I was looking forward to being a dentist. [*He advances hopefully towards the* NURSE]

NURSE [*hastily leaving the room too*] No, thank you very much.

MRS BROWN Come along, Paddington. [*She makes to leave*]

PADDINGTON [*examines Mr Leach's teeth with interest*] What a waste of good toffee. On the other hand, it's a good idea having detachable teeth. [*He follows* MRS BROWN *off*] If everyone had detachable teeth, there wouldn't be any need for dentists . . .

## CURTAIN

# Paddington Goes to the Launderette

# CAST OF CHARACTERS

MRS BIRD

PADDINGTON

LAUNDERETTE ATTENDANT

MR GRUBER

MR CURRY

## PROPS

Sheet of paper for list

Three laundry bags or pillowcases (two for Mrs Bird, one for Mr Gruber)

A pile of laundry – rags or old clothes

Pair of socks (normal size)

Pair of "shrunken" socks (baby size)

Pair of long combinations

*Pair of long combinations – enormously long

A few coins

Small packet (Paddington's sandwich)

Wheelbarrow

Four paper cups

Sign with instructions

*Three big cardboard boxes – two to be washing machines, one for the cocoa machine

Soap powder

Tray

Chairs

Magazine

Piece of wet bread (Paddington's soggy sandwich)

This is probably the most difficult play in the book and will need plenty of rehearsal if everything is to work at the right time. *Two cardboard packing cases with flaps cut into the tops will do for the washing machines. One of these boxes will have to be big enough for someone to hide inside. This person will have to throw out a soggy sandwich (p. 74) without being seen. If possible, there should be some sort of sound effect when the washing machine turns on (p. 73). This could be water sloshing in a bucket or a mechanical noise.

A third box will be needed for the cocoa machine, and this should be big enough to hide the person who will push the cocoa through an opening in the box. It should also have a coin slot. The two loud bangs can be made by thumping a tub or banging two tins together.

If you can't find a buzzer, a bicycle bell will do to sound the washing machine alarm, but the more noise the better! *Mr Curry's "stretched" long combinations could be cut from a sheet. They and the "shrunken" socks should be hidden in the washing machines before the play begins.

Instructions can be painted on cardboard and hung on the walls.

# Scene One

*[The Browns' sitting room.* MRS BIRD *is putting two piles of washing into bags and checking them against a list]*

MRS BIRD     Four pairs of socks, two woollen vests, one pair of long combinations . . .

PADDINGTON     *[enters]* Hullo, Mrs Bird.

MRS BIRD     Two shirts, four pillowcases, and one tablecloth. Hullo, Paddington. I must hurry, I want to catch the laundry man.

PADDINGTON     I'm afraid it's too late, Mrs Bird. He's already been. He went down the street about ten minutes ago.

MRS BIRD     There now! I asked him to call, he must have forgotten. Now what shall I do? These things *must* be washed today.

PADDINGTON     Would you like me to take them to the launderette, Mrs Bird?

MRS BIRD     I don't know. Launderettes are rather complicated.

PADDINGTON     I'm sure I could manage. Mr Gruber's told me about them. He says you just put the clothes in the machines, and then you sit and watch them going round and round. He says it's better than watching television.

MRS BIRD     Well, beggars can't be choosers, I suppose. I've got some of Mr Curry's things to take as well. He left them for the laundry man. Some socks and his long combinations.

PADDINGTON     I don't mind taking Mr Curry's clothes.

MRS BIRD      Are you sure you can manage?

PADDINGTON    Quite sure, Mrs Bird.

MRS BIRD      Well, here's some money. [*She hands it to him*] You'll find there's a cocoa machine in the launderette: if you put five pence into the slot, you'll get a good hot cup of cocoa so you can have your elevenses while the clothes are being washed.

PADDINGTON    Thank you very much, Mrs Bird.

MRS BIRD      And perhaps you would like to take this as well. [*She hands him a sandwich*]

PADDINGTON    [*putting it inside his hat*] Thank you, Mrs Bird.

MRS BIRD      Thank *you*, Paddington.

## Scene Two

[*The launderette. The* ATTENDANT *puts down her magazine as* PADDINGTON *comes through the door. He has the washing loose in a wheelbarrow*]

ATTENDANT     Come in, dear. My, you look as if you've got the washing for the whole street!

PADDINGTON    Oh, no, it's for Mrs Bird.

ATTENDANT     *Mrs* Bird? [*She holds up Mr Curry's long combinations*]

PADDINGTON    Yes. And Mr Curry, of course. [*He gives her a look*]

ATTENDANT     Oh, of course!

PADDINGTON    What do I have to do?

ATTENDANT   I'm afraid you'll need two machines for this lot. I'll give you number eleven and number twelve. You do know how to work them?

PADDINGTON   I think so.

ATTENDANT   Well, if you get into any trouble, the instructions are on the wall. [*She places four beakers of detergent on a nearby tray*] That's two beakers for each machine. You put the first lot in when it starts and the second lot when the buzzer sounds.

PADDINGTON   Thank you very much.

[*The* ATTENDANT *exits.* MR GRUBER *enters and collects his washing*]

MR GRUBER   Why, hullo Mr Brown. I didn't expect to see you here.

PADDINGTON   Hello, Mr Gruber, I'm very pleased to see you.

MR GRUBER   I've come to collect my washing. Is anything the matter?

PADDINGTON   I'm not sure which bundle of washing should go in the hot wash and which in the warm wash.

MR GRUBER   Oh, I expect I can help you there. [*He examines the bundles*] All of these go into the hot wash, and this bundle goes into the warm wash. [*He places them carefully*] The bundle on the *left* goes in the hot, and this bundle on the *right* goes into the warm. That's easy to remember, isn't it?

PADDINGTON   Oh yes, thank you. Left, hot. Right, warm.

MR GRUBER    You must get it the right way round or some
             will shrink and the others will stretch.

PADDINGTON   Have you finished your washing for today?

MR GRUBER    Oh, yes. I'm just leaving. Perhaps you
             would like to drop in for elevenses on your
             way home?

PADDINGTON   It's very kind of you, Mr Gruber, but I
             expect I'll get some cocoa from the machine.

MR GRUBER    Well, I'll have to get along and open the
             shop.

PADDINGTON   Goodbye, Mr Gruber. I'll see you soon, I
             hope.

MR GRUBER    Yes, goodbye, Mr Brown.

[PADDINGTON *switches on the washing machines. The
machine sound effects begin*]

PADDINGTON   Now, what did Mr Gruber say? Left, hot;
             right, warm. [*He walks over to the two bundles
             but looks at them from the other side so that left
             and right are reversed*] Left, hot. [*He puts it
             in the warm machine*] Right, warm. [*He puts
             the other bundle into the hot machine*] It's
             lucky that Mr Gruber came along. Now,
             what do I have to do? I know, put in one
             beaker of soap powder when the machine
             starts. [*He pours a carton of soap powder into
             the top of each machine*] That's right. Perhaps
             I'll have time for my elevenses before the
             buzzer sounds.

[*He crosses to the cocoa machine and puts a coin in the slot,
but no cocoa appears*]

             Oh, dear. It doesn't seem to be working.

[*He gives the machine a thump and immediately things start to happen. Cups of cocoa emerge through a hole in the front, one after another.* PADDINGTON *soon fills the tray, and they become mixed with the beakers of soap He tries to drink some in order to make room, but picks up a soap carton by mistake*]

Ugh! Soap!

[*He picks up the tray but at that moment the buzzer sounds. He is so confused that he starts emptying beakers of cocoa into the washing machines. There are two loud bangs from the machines.* PADDINGTON *lifts the lid of one of the machines, removes his hat and tries to blow away the steam. In doing so, his marmalade sandwich falls into the wash. He leans over and peers into the machine as* MR CURRY *enters.* MR CURRY *crosses and peers into the machine too*]

MR CURRY     Bear! What are you doing, bear?

[PADDINGTON *jumps out of the way and as he does so, something white and doughy flies out of the washing machine and hits* MR CURRY *in the face*]

Ugh! [*He wipes it off*] What on earth is this?

PADDINGTON   I think it's a marmalade sandwich, Mr Curry. I dropped one in by mistake.

MR CURRY     A marmalade sandwich? In a washing machine? Whatever next? And what's happened to my laundry? I heard you were doing it and I've come down to make sure it's all right.

PADDINGTON   I think it's ready now, Mr Curry. [*He opens the lid of the first machine*] Here are your socks.

[*He presents* MR CURRY *with the smallest pair of socks imaginable*]

MR CURRY     My *socks*? Look at them! They've shrunk. If you've done the same thing to my combinations, bear, I'll . . . I'll . . .

PADDINGTON   Oh, I don't think so, Mr Curry. They were in a different machine. [*He opens the door of the second machine*]

MR CURRY     Disgraceful! Give them here.
[*He grabs the ankles of the combinations as* PADDINGTON *pulls them out. They are now ten times as long as they were before. As* MR CURRY *spins across the launderette, they wrap themselves round him until he looks like an Egyptian mummy*]

PADDINGTON   You see, Mr Curry. I told you they wouldn't have shrunk.

MR CURRY     [*helpless*] Bear! Are you trying to take me for a ride?

PADDINGTON   [*comes up behind him with the wheelbarrow*] Take you for a ride? Certainly, Mr Curry!
[MR CURRY *falls over backwards into the wheelbarrow and is carried off at high speed by* PADDINGTON]

# CURTAIN

# Paddington Goes to the Hospital

# CAST OF CHARACTERS

MRS BROWN

MRS BIRD

PADDINGTON

NURSE

MR HEINZ, the psychiatrist

SIR ARCHIBALD, the doctor

MR CURRY

# PROPS

*In the Browns' sitting room:*
Chairs, table, etc.
Thermos
Basket
Fruit
*Cake with cherries on top
Letter
Paddington's hat

*In the hospital:*
Desk or table
Chairs
Toy telephone
Sheet of paper for list
Doctor's bag (toy bag or old handbag)
containing toy stethoscope and
hand mirror
White overall
*Operating mask
Pushchair
Blanket
Box of toy tools – hammer, chisel, saw, *mallet
Three white coats

The first scene takes place in the Browns' sitting room. For the rest of the play we need a small table, with a toy telephone and two chairs. There should be a long white overall for PADDINGTON to wear when he dresses up as the doctor and *a handkerchief (with loops to hook round the ears) for the operating mask. Any simple box will do for the tools. *The mallet, used to frighten MR CURRY (p. 91), can be a toy mallet, but the bigger it is the funnier it will be. You could make a big mallet by attaching a large tin can to a broom handle. It is *not* to be used, of course! A strong pushchair could serve as Mr Curry's wheelchair. The NURSE, SIR ARCHIBALD and MR HEINZ should wear white coats over their clothes.

PADDINGTON will also need a basket with some fruit, and if possible, a cake. *The cake doesn't have to be seen (it can stay in the basket), but if you do make one (real or imitation), be sure to put cherries on the top!

# Scene One

[*The Browns' sitting room.* MRS BROWN *is making up a basket of food when* MRS BIRD *comes in*]

MRS BROWN    If I see another bunch of grapes I shall scream. That's the third this week. Not to mention four pots of jam, two dozen eggs and a jar of calves-foot jelly.

MRS BIRD    I thought Mr Curry was supposed to be ill. He seems to have a very healthy appetite.

MRS BROWN    He says he hurt his leg in the launderette the other day. I don't know how long he'll be in hospital.

MRS BIRD    If you ask me, Mr Curry will be coming out of hospital when it suits *him* and not a minute before. He knows when he is on to a good thing. Free board and lodging.

MRS BROWN    And everybody at his beck and call.

MRS BIRD    He has a relapse every time the doctor says he is getting better. The Ward Sister has given him some strong hints that they're short of beds, but he takes no notice. And I'm certainly not having him staying here.

[PADDINGTON *comes in carrying a letter*]

PADDINGTON    There's a letter for you, Mrs Brown. It looks like Mr Curry's writing.

MRS BROWN    Yes, I'm afraid you're right. [*She opens the envelope*]

MRS BIRD    What does he say?

MRS BROWN  [*reading*] Dear Mrs Brown, my leg is still troubling me. Will you please send some more apples. I didn't like the last lot – they were too sour. Also another cherry cake. P.S. Two cherries were missing from the one you sent last week.

PADDINGTON  [*guiltily*] Perhaps they were a bit loose?

MRS BIRD  [*with meaning*] Perhaps!

MRS BROWN  P.P.S. I would like them as soon as possible. Paddington could bring them round to the hospital . . . Do you mind taking this parcel to him, Paddington?

PADDINGTON  [*cheerfully*] No. I don't think I've ever been to a hospital before. I wonder if it's like the Daredevil Doctor series on television?

MRS BIRD  I shouldn't think so for one moment.

MRS BROWN  There now. It's packed. And I've fixed the cherries *firmly* in the cake this time, so let's hope they don't fall out.

MRS BIRD  I've packed you some sandwiches and a thermos flask of cocoa. But be careful, it's very hot.

PADDINGTON  Thank you Mrs Bird. I won't be long. [*He puts on his hat as he goes out*]

MRS BROWN  I do hope we're doing the right thing, letting him go by himself.

MRS BIRD  I shouldn't worry about that bear. He knows how to look after number one.

MRS BROWN  It wasn't Paddington I was thinking of, it's the hospital . . .

81

# Scene Two

[*A small room in the hospital. A* NURSE *sits at the desk with a telephone. She is finishing a conversation*]

NURSE        Yes, Sir Archibald. Very good, Sir Archibald.

[*She replaces the phone as* PADDINGTON *knocks at the door*]

       Come in.

PADDINGTON        Good morning.

NURSE        Good morning. Can I help you?

PADDINGTON        I've come to see Mr Curry.

NURSE        [*looking through a list*] Mr Curry . . . have you any idea what he does?

PADDINGTON        He grumbles a lot.

NURSE        That doesn't help. I think I'd better pass you on to the person who deals with enquiries.

PADDINGTON        Thank you very much. Is he the head man?

NURSE        The *head* man. Bless me! Why didn't you say so before? You want the doctor who looks after things up here. [*She taps her head*]

PADDINGTON        Up here? [*He taps his own head*].

NURSE        Yes. He's what we call the head shrinker.

PADDINGTON        My hat *is* a bit tight. But I don't think I want my head shrunk. Couldn't you stretch my hat instead?

NURSE        Stretch your hat?

PADDINGTON    Yes. If it was a bit bigger I could carry more sandwiches in it.

NURSE    [*leaning across the desk*] Sandwiches?

PADDINGTON    [*leaning across the desk so that they are nose-to-nose*] Yes, but I would still have to find somewhere for my cocoa.

NURSE    [*alarmed*] There, there. There's nothing to worry about. [*Picks up the phone quickly and dials a number*] Mr Heinz, could you come quickly, please? There's a patient who needs you urgently. Thank you. [*Replaces the phone*]

PADDINGTON    Mr Heinz! I don't want to see Mr Heinz, I want to see Mr Curry. I've brought him one of Mrs Bird's cherry cakes.

NURSE    [*soothingly*] I think you'll find Mr Heinz much nicer. He'll soon take your worries away. [MR HEINZ *enters*] Oh, Mr Heinz, I'm so glad to see you. [*She looks at* PADDINGTON *and taps her head*] There's the patient. [*She hurries out*]

PADDINGTON    Patient? Have I got long to wait?

MR HEINZ    Oh, no, in fact I'll start right away. Just open your coat, please.

PADDINGTON    I'm sorry about the cherry cake.

MR HEINZ    [*taking off his glasses and staring at* PADDINGTON] You are sorry about the *cherry cake*?

PADDINGTON    Yes. I wish I could give you a slice but Mr Curry would only complain. I can give you one of my marmalade sandwiches.

MR HEINZ          [*a slight shudder*] No, thank you. Now, I'd
                  like to play a little game. It's really to test
                  your reactions. [*He sits down in a chair by
                  his desk*]

PADDINGTON        A game to test my reactions? I didn't know
                  I had any.

MR HEINZ          Oh, yes. [*He puts his feet up on another
                  chair*] Everybody has reactions. Some have
                  fast ones and some have slow. [PAD-
                  DINGTON *sits on his feet*] Oooh!

PADDINGTON        I'm sorry, Mr Heinz.

MR HEINZ          Now, I'm going to call out some words –
                  quite quickly – and each time I call one
                  out, I want you to give me another word
                  which has the opposite meaning ...
                  right?

PADDINGTON        [*promptly, as he settles down in the other
                  chair*] Wrong.

MR HEINZ          What's the matter? Aren't you com-
                  fortable?

PADDINGTON        Oh, yes, but you told me to say the
                  opposite every time you gave me a
                  word.

MR HEINZ          That wasn't the word, bear! Wait until
                  I give you the go ahead. Once you start
                  I don't want to hear anything else.
                  Ready ... Three ... two ... one ... go!

PADDINGTON        Stop!

MR HEINZ          What's the matter?

PADDINGTON        You said "go" so I said "stop".

| | |
|---|---|
| MR HEINZ | Oh. Very good. |
| PADDINGTON | Very bad. |
| MR HEINZ | Look here! |
| PADDINGTON | Look there! [*A pause*] Can't you think of any more words, Mr Heinz? |
| MR HEINZ | [*drums his fingers on the desk for a moment then decides to try again*] White. |
| PADDINGTON | Black. |
| MR HEINZ | Big. |
| PADDINGTON | Small. |
| MR HEINZ | Fast. |
| PADDINGTON | Slow. |
| MR HEINZ | Dark. |
| PADDINGTON | Light. |
| MR HEINZ | Fine. |
| PADDINGTON | Wet. |
| MR HEINZ | That's good. We've finished. |
| PADDINGTON | That's bad. We've started. |
| MR HEINZ | No, we haven't! |
| PADDINGTON | Yes, we have! |
| MR HEINZ | [*thumping table*] No . . . no . . . no! |
| PADDINGTON | [*thumps the table too, in his excitement*] Yes . . . yes . . . yes! |
| MR HEINZ | [*yelling*] Will you stop! |
| PADDINGTON | No, I won't! |
| MR HEINZ | [*his head in his hands*] Why did I ever take this up? I should have my head examined. |

PADDINGTON     [*sitting up*] Perhaps it needs shrinking. I should go and talk to the nurse who was here a few minutes ago. She might be able to help you. She knows all about those things.

[*As* PADDINGTON *gets up,* MR HEINZ *makes a dash for the door*]

MR HEINZ     I shall be gone for five minutes. Five minutes! And if you're still here when I get back . . . I'll . . . I'll . . . [*He hurries out, at a loss for words*]

PADDINGTON     [*looking round the room*] What a funny hospital. It's not at all like the one in Daredevil Doctor. It must be time for elevenses. I'm glad Mrs Brown remembered to give me some cocoa. [*He fills the thermos cup and takes a mouthful*] Ow! [*He hops round the room in agony*] Ooh! [*He picks up a doctor's bag from the corner of the room, opens it and examines his tongue in a mirror*] I knew it, I've blistered my tongue . . . [*He becomes interested in the contents of the bag*] What's this? [*He puts on a stethoscope and listens to his own heart*] Hmm. I wonder what it's like to be a doctor.

[*He slips on a white gown and hangs the stethoscope round his neck*]

[*As a television surgeon*] Nurse! Instruments ready? All right, bring in the patient. [*He puts on his operating mask and paces up and down*] Now this is serious . . .

[*The* NURSE *comes in suddenly*]

| | |
|---|---|
| NURSE | It certainly is serious. Sir Archibald is coming. |
| PADDINGTON | Is he? |
| NURSE | And he's in a terrible mood. You know he doesn't like students who aren't punctual. |
| PADDINGTON | Student? But I'm not . . . |
| NURSE | He's here now. I'd say I'm sorry straight away, if I were you. |
| SIR ARCHIBALD | [storming in] Ah, there you are. |
| PADDINGTON | Good morning, Sir Archibald. I'm sorry, Sir Archibald! |
| SIR ARCHIBALD | Sorry? I should think so! Good afternoon's more like it! Now you *are* here, perhaps you can give us the benefit of your advice. I'd like to have your diagnosis. |
| PADDINGTON | My diagnosis! [*He begins to unload his basket*] There's a cherry cake, some eggs, some calves-foot jelly, but I don't think Mrs Brown packed a diagnosis. |
| SIR ARCHIBALD | Calves-foot jelly. Did you say *calves-foot jelly*? |
| PADDINGTON | Yes. Grant Dexter says it's very good if you're ill. |
| SIR ARCHIBALD | Grant Dexter! And who might he be? |
| PADDINGTON | You don't know Grant Dexter? He's the Daredevil Doctor. He's very good at curing people. All his patients get better. |
| SIR ARCHIBALD | Are you suggesting mine don't, doctor . . . whatever your name is? |

87

PADDINGTON   Doctor? I'm not a doctor, Sir Archibald. [*He pulls off his mask*] I'm a bear. I've come to visit Mr Curry.

SIR ARCHIBALD   [*on the point of exploding*] Curry? Did you say Curry?

PADDINGTON   That's right.

SIR ARCHIBALD   Are you a friend of his?

PADDINGTON   Well, I'm not really a friend. He lives next door and I've brought him some food to be going on with.

SIR ARCHIBALD   Food! That's the last thing he needs. It will only make him stay longer. That man's entirely without scruples.

PADDINGTON   Mr Curry's without scruples! I thought he'd only hurt his leg!

SIR ARCHIBALD   Scruples, bear, are things that stop some people taking advantage of others.

PADDINGTON   Oh. I don't think Mr Curry's got any of those, Sir Archibald. Mrs Bird's always grumbling because he takes advantage of others.

SIR ARCHIBALD   I see. [*Thoughtfully*] Are you any good at tricks, bear?

PADDINGTON   Oh, yes, Sir Archibald. Bears are very good at tricks.

SIR ARCHIBALD   I thought you might be. Nurse, wheel Mr Curry in here, we'll see him privately.

[*The* NURSE *goes and* SIR ARCHIBALD *turns to* PADDINGTON]

   I think it's time we gave Mr Curry a

surprise – and I think you're the one to give it. Now, if you'll just put your mask back on, bear . . .

PADDINGTON     Yes, Sir Archibal d. [*He does*]

SIR ARCHIBALD     I'll give you a chance to see what it's like to be – what did you say his name was?

PADDINGTON     Grant Dexter. The Daredevil Doctor.

SIR ARCHIBALD     Now I've had an idea. [*He goes to the door and returns with a tool box*] The workmen left these when they were doing some repairs. When I tell you to get your instruments ready, this is the box I want you to take them from.

PADDINGTON     Right, Sir Archibald.

[MR CURRY *arrives in a wheelchair pushed by the* NURSE]

SIR ARCHIBALD     Good morning, Mr Curry.

MR CURRY     [*overdoing the agony*] Oooooooh!

SIR ARCHIBALD     How's the patient today?

MR CURRY     Worse, much worse.

SIR ARCHIBALD     [*cheerfully*] I thought you might be, that's why we have decided to operate.

MR CURRY     [*sitting up quickly*] Operate? Did you say operate?

SIR ARCHIBALD     Yes, that's right. No good playing around with these things. I'd like to introduce you to . . . a colleague from overseas. He specializes in legs. Does something or other to the knee. Nobody quite knows what, but it seems to work very well in the jungle. Quite a few of his patients

89

still manage to get about after a fashion. [*To* PADDINGTON] Perhaps you'd like to listen to the patient's heart?

PADDINGTON  Of course, Sir Archibald. [*He sticks the stethoscope under the blanket*]

SIR ARCHIBALD  What can you hear?

PADDINGTON  It's got a very strong beat [*He jumps up and down to the rhythm*] I think it's Pick of the Pops.

MR CURRY  Pick of the Pops! You've got your stethoscope on my transistor radio!

PADDINGTON  I'm sorry, Mr Curry. [*In his confusion he reverses the stethoscope and puts the headpiece on* MR CURRY. *He shouts in the other end*] Are you there?

[MR CURRY *jumps*]

MR CURRY  Of course I am! [*He turns to* SIR ARCHIBALD] Is this . . . this *person* going to be allowed to operate on me? He's not big enough for a start.

SIR ARCHIBALD  [*calmly*] Oh, don't worry about his size. We'll give him a box to stand on.

MR CURRY  A box to stand on!

SIR ARCHIBALD  Yes, it may make him a bit wobbly but it'll be all right.

MR CURRY  What!

SIR ARCHIBALD  [*he turns to* PADDINGTON *with a wink*] Now, if you would just like to get your instruments ready.

PADDINGTON    Certainly, Sir Archibald. [*He opens the carpenter's tool box*] One hammer ... [*He puts it on the desk*]

MR CURRY    A hammer!

PADDINGTON    One chisel. [*He puts it next to the hammer*]

MR CURRY    A chisel!

PADDINGTON    And one saw. [*He brings out a large carpenter's saw*]

MR CURRY    A saw!

SIR ARCHIBALD    How about something to put him to sleep with, nurse?

[*The* NURSE *hands* PADDINGTON *an enormous mallet*]

MR CURRY    I'm off. [*He leaps out of the chair*]

SIR ARCHIBALD    Ah, Mr Curry, I'm glad you're feeling better. You can leave the hospital today.

MR CURRY    Leave? I don't know what you're talking about.

SIR ARCHIBALD    You aren't limping any more, Mr Curry. In fact, I would say you are completely cured.

MR CURRY    [*realizes he's been beaten*] Bah! [*He storms out*]

SIR ARCHIBALD    [*after his laughter has subsided*] It seems we have another free bed in the ward after all, nurse. [*He removes Paddington's mask and shakes his paw warmly*] Congratulations, bear. I've never in all my life seen a patient recover so quickly. Perhaps you would like to keep your stethoscope as a souvenir?

PADDINGTON    Thank you very much, Sir Archibald. [*He picks up his basket*] Would you like some of this cake? I don't suppose Mr Curry will be needing it now.

SIR ARCHIBALD    Mmm. It does seem rather a pity to waste it. [*He looks over his shoulder to make sure the nurse can't hear and then lowers his voice*] Do you like the cherries?

PADDINGTON    [*lowers his voice too*] I think they're the best part. Except Mrs Bird's put them on extra tightly this time.

SIR ARCHIBALD    [*reaches for the tool box*] I don't doubt we'll find something to lever them off with. [*He hands* PADDINGTON *a suitable tool*] After you . . .

PADDINGTON    No, after you, Sir Archibald.

[*Together, they dig into the basket*]

# CURTAIN

# Paddington Turns Detective

# CAST OF CHARACTERS

MR BROWN

MRS BROWN

MRS BIRD

PADDINGTON

MR GRUBER

POLICEMAN

MR CURRY

JUDY

JONATHAN

# PROPS

*In the Browns' sitting room:*
Table, chairs, etc.
Paddington's hat
Torch
Sandwich
Plastic clothes line
Battery
Pillowcase
Lantern

*In Mr Gruber's shop:*
Chairs, bric-a-brac, etc.
Book
Cardboard box containing a magnifying glass,
whistle, some small bottles, a pad of paper, and a
false beard (could be made of yarn or cotton wool)
Large old coat

*At Paddington Station:*
Luggage and parcels
"Paddington Station" sign
Jar of marmalade
Photo-frame with picture of Aunt Lucy (with glass,
if possible)

For the best effect this play needs to be performed after dark, or at least with the curtains drawn. Much of the action takes place at midnight, outside the Browns' house. It should not be necessary to change the scene: simply use the back part of the stage for the sitting room and the front part for the out-of-doors scene. This scene will be funnier if the BROWNS and MRS BIRD appear in their nightclothes – but this is a matter of choice.

PADDINGTON will need a simple detective outfit (a beard, a magnifying glass and a whistle are the most important items) and MRS BROWN should have a torch battery, plastic clothes line and a sandwich ready to give him before he goes to his room. You will also need an alarm clock for sound effects. Paddington Station is exactly the same as we saw it when Paddington arrived in the first play p. 14. The station announcement can be made by somebody speaking loudly into a bucket or tin basin.

The POLICEMAN should wear something that looks like a uniform. He can wear a toy helmet, or one that has been made of cardboard with a milkbottle top for the badge. He also needs a notepad and pencil.

## Scene One

[*The Browns' sitting room.* MR *and* MRS BROWN *are talking*]

MR BROWN  I can't think who would do a thing like that.

MRS BROWN  Nor can I, Henry, it's never happened before.

MR BROWN  I suppose it's too late to do anything about it now. It's very disappointing.

MRS BIRD  [*coming in from the kitchen*] What's the matter, Mr Brown?

MR BROWN  Someone's stolen my prize marrow.

MRS BIRD  When did that happen?

MR BROWN  I don't know for sure. It was there on Wednesday. They must have stolen it during the night.

MRS BIRD  [*after exchanging a look with Mrs Brown*] Well, you've got several more.

[PADDINGTON *comes in*]

MR BROWN  That isn't the point.

PADDINGTON  Good morning, everybody.

MRS BIRD  Good morning, Paddington.

PADDINGTON  Is anything the matter, Mr Brown?

MR BROWN  Somebody has stolen my prize marrow. I've several more, of course, but they'll never be ready in time for the show.

PADDINGTON  Oh, dear! I'm sorry to hear that, Mr Brown.

MR BROWN       It's the biggest I've ever grown. I felt I was
               sure to win a prize. I've a good mind to offer
               a reward to anybody who tracks down the
               culprit. [*A thoughtful look comes into* PAD-
               DINGTON'S *eye and he makes for the door*]

MRS BROWN      Aren't you having any breakfast this
               morning, Paddington?

PADDINGTON     No, thank you, Mrs Brown. I want to see
               Mr Gruber about something.

MRS BROWN      What's that?

PADDINGTON     I'm not sure until I see him. [*He puts on his
               hat and goes*]

MR BROWN       *Now* what has he got on his mind?

MRS BIRD       I don't know, but I noticed a funny look
               came into his eyes when you mentioned a
               reward . . .

## Scene Two

[*Mr Gruber's shop.* MR GRUBER *puts down the book he is
reading as* PADDINGTON *comes in*]

PADDINGTON     Good morning, Mr Gruber.

MR GRUBER      Good morning, Mr Brown. You're early
               today. It's only ten o'clock.

PADDINGTON     Yes. I've got a problem and I wondered if
               you could help me.

MR GRUBER      I'll do my best. Tell me about it.

PADDINGTON     It's a flashing light.

MR GRUBER      A flashing light?

PADDINGTON   In the garden at Number thirty-two, Windsor Gardens – and Mr Brown's marrow.

MR GRUBER   You'd better begin at the beginning.

PADDINGTON   Yes, I suppose I had. You see, I've got a new torch and last night, when I was in bed, I shone it at the window by mistake. Then I noticed that somebody was flashing a light outside in the garden – like a signal. So I flashed my light on and off three times and the light outside the window flashed three times as well.

MR GRUBER   What did you do?

PADDINGTON   I pulled the bedclothes over my head and went to sleep!

MR GRUBER   I see.

PADDINGTON   Then, when I came down to breakfast this morning, Mr Brown told me that somebody had stolen his prize marrow.

MR GRUBER   And you think that the two things are connected?

PADDINGTON   That's right, and I thought I would like to catch whoever it is. Not just for the reward . . .

MR GRUBER   [twinkling] Oh, there's a reward, is there?

PADDINGTON   [casually] Mr Brown did mention it. Do you remember that book you showed me once about the famous detective?

MR GRUBER   Sherlock Holmes? Yes.

PADDINGTON   I would like to be able to catch criminals like he did. But I may need to disguise myself. It'll make things a lot easier.

MR GRUBER    I think I can help you there, Mr Brown. [*He takes down a cardboard box*] Somebody sold this to me a long time ago. You can borrow it if you like.

PADDINGTON    [*reading from the lid of the box*] Master Detective's Disguise Outfit. Thank you very much, Mr Gruber. May I look inside?

MR GRUBER    Of course.

PADDINGTON    It looks very interesting. [*He takes out a magnifying glass*] What's this, Mr Gruber?

MR GRUBER    That's a magnifying glass to look for clues.

PADDINGTON    Very useful. And here's a police-whistle and some bottles and a pad.

MR GRUBER    They're for fingerprints and one of the bottles is full of invisible ink.

PADDINGTON    And a beard! Just what I need.

MR GRUBER    Here. Try this old coat. It may be a bit big. [PADDINGTON *slips it on. It trails behind him*]

PADDINGTON    Thank you very much, Mr Gruber. [*He hooks the beard over his ears*] How's that?

MR GRUBER    Splendid!

PADDINGTON    [*putting his bush hat on*] I don't think anybody will recognize me now.

MR GRUBER    [*as Doctor Watson*] Do you think it will be a difficult crime to solve, Mr Holmes?

PADDINGTON    On the contrary, elementary, my dear Watson. [*He tucks the disguise outfit under his arm and sails out*]

## Scene Three

[*The living room at Number thirty-two, Windsor Gardens. There is a knock on the door.* MRS BIRD *goes to answer it*]

PADDINGTON [*in a deep voice*] Good morning.

MRS BIRD Oh, hello, Paddington. I didn't expect you back so quickly.

PADDINGTON I'm not Paddington, Mrs Bird. I'm Sherlock Holmes – the famous detective.

MRS BIRD Yes dear. Don't forget to wipe your feet.

MRS BROWN [*coming in from the kitchen*] Is Paddington back already? I thought he would be having his elevenses with Mr Gruber.

MRS BIRD He's up to something, but I don't know what. He's just come back in a long over-coat, hidden behind a beard like Father Christmas, and he looked very thoughtful.

MRS BROWN Oh, dear! Something always happens when he's like that.

[PADDINGTON *enters minus his disguise*]

PADDINGTON Hullo, Mrs Brown.

MRS BROWN Hallo, Paddington.

PADDINGTON I wonder if I could have a new battery for my torch?

MRS BROWN Is the other one flat already?

PADDINGTON Yes. I've had to use it rather a lot lately.

MRS BROWN Here you are.

PADDINGTON Thank you very much, Mrs Brown. [*He goes into the hall*]

MRS BIRD    I wonder why he needs his torch? [PAD-DINGTON *comes back suddenly, making them jump*]

PADDINGTON    Mrs Brown, do you happen to have some rope I could borrow?

MRS BROWN    I don't think I have any rope but I've a plastic clothes line. Would that be any good?

PADDINGTON    [*gravely*] That would do very well.

MRS BIRD    Here you are. [*Gives him the clothes line*]

PADDINGTON    Thank you. [*He goes into the hall again*]

MRS BIRD    And what does he need those things for?

MRS BROWN    I shudder to think.

PADDINGTON    [*coming back suddenly again*] There's just one more thing.

MRS BIRD    [*wearily*] Yes, Paddington?

PADDINGTON    I wonder if I could take my elevenses to my room today. I'm not very hungry at the moment, and I may feel like a marmalade sandwich later.

MRS BROWN    Here you are, all ready and waiting for you. [*She hands him the sandwiches on a plate*]

PADDINGTON    Thank you very much. [*He goes off as* MRS BROWN *and* MRS BIRD *shake their heads in amazement. After a moment they go off too*]

[*Blackout. After a moment the alarm clock sounds in the distance*]

[PADDINGTON *yawns as he enters*] Midnight, that's the best time to catch criminals.

[*He switches on his torch and shines it through the window*] Nothing there, but I'd better be prepared. [*He puts on his beard, overcoat and hat and picks up his case*] I'll go and hide in the greenhouse. [*He goes off. A moment later, a shadowy figure appears at the front of the stage. He is carrying a lantern, but is muffled up in a scarf so we don't see his face. As he reaches the front door,* PADDINGTON *comes along carrying the clothes line and pillowcase. The figure walks away and* PADDINGTON *creeps up behind him. The figure turns round suddenly, but* PADDINGTON *ducks and isn't noticed. The next time the figure turns away,* PADDINGTON *seizes his opportunity, pops the pillowcase and lassoo over his head and runs round him with the clothes line, pinning his arms to his sides so that he can't remove the pillowcase. When he is secured,* PADDINGTON *blows his whistle*]

It's no good struggling. You've met your match! [*The figure answers with a muffled snort and struggles to get free*] Be quiet, you will have your chance to speak when the police get here.

[PADDINGTON *leads him indoors just as the* POLICE-MAN *arrives on the scene*]

POLICEMAN    Hullo. Hullo. What's going on here?

PADDINGTON   Good evening, Officer, that was quick.

POLICEMAN    I just happened to be passing, sir, and I heard your whistle. What's the trouble?

PADDINGTON   I've captured a burglar! I think he's the one who took Mr Brown's marrow.

POLICEMAN   Mr Brown's marrow?

PADDINGTON   That's right. I thought I saw a flashing light. Then I saw a shadowy figure. I couldn't see his face but from the way he walked, I'm sure it had a nasty look on it.

POLICEMAN   Well sir, let's see, shall we? I'll switch the light on. [*He switches on the light and then jerks the rope which* PADDINGTON *has been holding. The figure spins round until he comes to the end of it. The* POLICEMAN *undoes the lassoo and the figure wrenches the pillowcase from his head*]

PADDINGTON   Oh, dear! [*He puts his torch down*]

MR CURRY   What is the meaning of this assault?

POLICEMAN   [*to* PADDINGTON] You were right. He *has* got a nasty look on his face. You are accused of acting in a suspicious manner.

MR CURRY   Suspicious manner! I was going about my own business.

POLICEMAN   At midnight? With a lantern?

MR CURRY   I happen to collect moths and the light of the lantern attracts them. [*He suddenly sees* PADDINGTON] Bear! I might have known you would be at the bottom of this.

PADDINGTON   I'm sorry, Mr Curry. [*He takes off his beard*]

MR CURRY   Not as sorry as you will be!

POLICEMAN   Hmmm. And what were you doing prowling round the house in disguise, young fellow-me-bear?

[MR *and* MRS BROWN, *awakened by the din, come onstage*]

| | |
|---|---|
| POLICEMAN | Unless you can explain yourself . . . |
| MR BROWN | Whatever is the matter? |
| PADDINGTON | Well, I'm afraid it's a bit complicated. You see, it all happened because of your marrow, Mr Brown . . . The one you were getting ready for the show. I was trying to catch the thief. |
| MR BROWN | I don't see how my marrow has anything to do with this noise. |
| MRS BROWN | I think I'm beginning to understand . . . Paddington was trying to catch the person who took it. But I'm afraid he didn't stand a chance. |
| POLICEMAN | Why not, madam? |
| MRS BROWN | I was going to tell you sooner or later, Henry. It's my fault really, you see . . . I cut your marrow by mistake! |
| MR BROWN | You did? You cut my prize marrow? |
| MRS BROWN | Well, I didn't realize it was your prize one. And you know how fond you are of stuffed marrow. We had it for dinner on Thursday. |
| MR BROWN | We had it for dinner? How could you? |
| POLICEMAN | Here, not so fast, sir, I can't get it all down. Has anybody else anything to say? |
| MR CURRY | Yes, I have. I demand that this bear is punished. Springing out on an innocent member of the public. I shall demand damages. [PADDINGTON *is very unhappy at the trouble that he has caused. He decides to creep quietly away before anybody notices*] |

POLICEMAN     [*to* MR BROWN] What do you say to that, sir?

MR BROWN     As my marrow seems to have caused all this trouble, perhaps I had better try to find a solution to the problem. This morning I promised a reward to anybody who found out who took the marrow. Now, through you, Mr Curry, we have actually found the culprit. [MRS BROWN *looks guilty*] Suppose I gave the reward to *you*. Would that satisfy you?

MR CURRY     Well, I don't know . . .

MR BROWN     Say five pounds?

MR CURRY     [*after a moment's hesitation*] Very well, but it mustn't happen again. And I demand an apology.

MR BROWN     I'm sure Paddington didn't mean any harm, but, of course, he will apologize.

MRS BROWN     Where is he?

[JUDY *and* JONATHAN, *who have appeared by this time, begin to look for him*]

MRS BIRD     [*enters*] Whatever is going on here?

JUDY     It's Paddington. He's missing.

JONATHAN     He isn't in his room. I've just looked in there.

JUDY     And all his things have gone.

JONATHAN     His suitcase . . .

JUDY     His clothes . . . and his picture of Aunt Lucy . . .

JONATHAN     Everything!

| | |
|---|---|
| MRS BROWN | Where on earth can he have got to? |
| MR BROWN | There's only one thing for it, we must organize a search party. [*He picks up the torch*] |
| MRS BROWN | But where can we look? We don't even know where to start. |
| MRS BIRD | [*grimly, as she puts on her coat*] I do . . . follow me. If you want my opinion, there isn't a moment to lose. |

[MRS BIRD *hurries out followed by the rest of the family*]

| | |
|---|---|
| MR CURRY | Hey! Hold on! Wait for me! [*He hurries after them*] |

## Scene Four

[*Paddington Station. It is set as in the first play, p. 15, with luggage and parcels. There is an announcement over the tannoy "The train about to leave from Platform One is the Boat-train Special". A Guard's whistle sounds. The* BROWNS *rush across stage, but the train is already moving off. A moment later they walk sadly back on*]

| | |
|---|---|
| JUDY | Too late! |
| MR BROWN | We don't *know* he was on it. |
| JONATHAN | I bet he was. I bet Mrs Bird was right. |
| JUDY | She usually is. Besides, you heard what they said . . . |
| JONATHAN | It was the Boat-train Special! |
| MRS BROWN | Goodness knows where he'll end up. |
| MRS BIRD | [*following on behind*] If only I'd thought of it before. |

| | |
|---|---|
| JUDY | Can't we ring up the station at the other end? |
| MR BROWN | We can. But knowing Paddington, he might get off anywhere. |
| MRS BIRD | Things just won't be the same without that bear. |
| MR BROWN | You can say that again! |

[*He turns to leave, and as he does so,* PADDINGTON *pops up from behind the parcels and raises his hat.* MR BROWN *sees him and shines the torch in his direction*]

| | |
|---|---|
| | Paddington! |
| PADDINGTON | Hullo, Mr Brown. |
| THE BROWNS | [*chorus*] Paddington! |
| JUDY | You didn't go after all! |
| PADDINGTON | I did. But I missed the train. I seem to cause so much trouble that I thought you wouldn't want me to stay any more, so I thought I'd better go back to Darkest Peru. |

[*He reaches behind the parcels and takes a jar of marmalade, which he puts in his suitcase. Then he holds up his picture of Aunt Lucy.*]

| | |
|---|---|
| | I haven't even had time to pack properly. |
| MRS BROWN | Not want you to stay? |
| MRS BIRD | Of course, we want you to stay. |
| JUDY | Even Mr Curry wants you to stay. Don't you, Mr Curry? |
| MR CURRY | Well, er . . . Hmmmmmmmph. |
| MR BROWN | [*waving his torch in the direction of Paddington's photograph frame as he talks*] Besides, if you go, who's going to eat all the marmalade? |

MRS BIRD          Exactly! The cupboard's full.

PADDINGTON        [*peering at the glass on the photograph excitedly*] Would you mind doing that again, Mr Brown?

MR BROWN          Do what again?

PADDINGTON        Wave your torch about.

MR BROWN          You mean . . . like that? [*He repeats the action*]

PADDINGTON        That's it! That's what I saw the other night! Oh, dear!

JUDY              Can anyone join in?

JONATHAN          Or is it a secret?

PADDINGTON        It's a reflection, Mr Brown. You see, when I shone that torch at my bedroom window the other night, I thought I saw someone signalling back at me. Only it wasn't . . . I thought it was the man who'd stolen your marrow. But it must have been the reflection from my own torch all the time . . .

MRS BROWN         [*looks at the others*] Paddington . . .

PADDINGTON        Yes, Mrs Brown?

MRS BROWN         You're incorrigible!

PADDINGTON        [*hotly*] I'm not, Mrs Brown. I'm a bear!

JUDY              And a jolly good bear at that. [*She takes his paw*]

JONATHAN          Hear! Hear! [*nudges Judy, takes Paddington's other paw, and together they lift him onto a box. Cue for song. JONATHAN and JUDY lead the others into "For He's a Jolly Good Bear Cub" as the play ends*]

## CURTAIN

# Songs

# I Try So Hard

PADDINGTON  I try so hard to get things right,
So why do things go wrong?
When I paint the ceiling, people stop and stare
Just because the whitewash gets into my hair.

AUDIENCE  I try so hard to get things right,
So why do things go wrong?

PADDINGTON  When I help the plumber, I feel such a fool,
What was once the kitchen, is now a swimming pool.

AUDIENCE  I try so hard to get things right,
So why do things go wrong?

PADDINGTON  When I do the cooking, why do people joke?
Just because the last lot all went up in smoke.

AUDIENCE  I try so hard to get things right,
So why do things go wrong?

PADDINGTON  People mock my gardening, when I'm planting seeds.
Pulling up the carrots, watering the weeds.

AUDIENCE  I try so hard to get things right,
So why do things go wrong?

PADDINGTON  Whenever there's a problem, I try to lend a paw,
But things always end up much worse than before.

ALL  I try so hard to get things right,
So why do things go wrong?

## Paddington Bear

He's here, he's there, he's Paddington Bear,
A rare sort of bear from Peru.
Paddington, Paddington, Paddington, there
Will never be another like you.

Cocoa in his thermos,
Sandwich in his hat,
Always pleased to greet you,
Likes to have an elevenses chat.
When you're next in London,
Look around and there
You will find a station
That has been named after this bear.

He's here, he's there, he's Paddington Bear,
A rare sort of bear from Peru.
Paddington, Paddington, Paddington, there
Will never be another like you.

Paddington's adventures
Drive our cares away,
He turns frowns to smiles and
Makes work seem a holiday.
He likes making toffee
For us all to share,
He sticks to his friends and
They stick to this marmalade bear.

He's here, he's there, he's Paddington Bear,
A rare sort of bear from Peru.
Paddington, Paddington, Paddington, there
Will never be another like you.

Paddington's adventures
Never seem to end,
Everybody loves him,
He's our very own favourite friend.
Life was very quiet till
He changed everything,
But we all enjoy it,
That is why we smile when we sing,

He's here, he's there, he's Paddington Bear,
A rare sort of bear from Peru.
Paddington, Paddington, Paddington, there
Will never be another like you.